Ghosteria

Volume One: the Stories

Ghosteria

Volume One: The Stories

Tanith Lee

Stafford England

Ghosteria
Volume One: The Stories
By Tanith Lee
© 2014

This is a work of fiction. All the characters and events portrayed in this book are fictitious, and any resemblance to real people, or events, is purely coincidental.

All rights reserved, including the right to reproduce this book, or portions thereof, in any form.

The right of Tanith Lee to be identified as the author of this work has been asserted by her in accordance with the Copyright, Design and Patents Act, 1988.

Cover by Danielle Lainton & Storm Constantine from an idea by Tanith Lee
Layout by Storm Constantine
Set in Palatino Linotype

ISBN 978-1-907737-61-9

IP0118

New (future) Author Web Site, as the original has been stolen:
http://www.tanith-lee.com

An Immanion Press Edition
http://www.immanion-press.com
info@immanion-press.com

Books by Tanith Lee

A Selection from her 93 titles

The Birthgrave Trilogy (The Birthgrave; Vazkor, son of Vazkor, Quest for the White Witch)
The Vis Trilogy (The Storm Lord; Anackire; The White Serpent)
The Flat Earth Opus (Night's Master; Death's Master; Delusion's Master; Delirium's Mistress; Night's Sorceries)
Don't Bite the Sun
Drinking Sapphire Wine
The Paradys Quartet (The Book of the Damned; The Book of the Beast; The Book of the Dead; The Book of the Mad)
The Venus Quartet (Faces Under Water; Saint Fire; A Bed of Earth; Venus Preserved)
Sung in Shadow
A Heroine of the World
The Scarabae Blood Opera (Dark Dance; Personal Darkness; Darkness, I)
The Blood of Roses
When the Lights Go Out
Heart-Beast
Elephantasm
Reigning Cats and Dogs
The Unicorn Trilogy (Black Unicorn; Gold Unicorn; Red Unicorn)
The Claidi Journals (Law of the Wolf Tower; Wolf Star Rise, Queen of the Wolves, Wolf Wing)
The Piratica Novels (Piratica 1; Piratica 2; Piratica 3)
The Silver Metal Lover
Metallic Love
The Gods Are Thirsty

Collections

Nightshades
Dreams of Dark and Light
Red As Blood – Tales From the Sisters Grimmer
Tamastara, or the Indian Nights
The Gorgon
Tempting the Gods
Hunting the Shadows
Sounds and Furies

Also Published by Immanion Press
The Colouring Book Series

Greyglass
To Indigo
L'Amber
Killing Violets
Ivoria
Cruel Pink
Turquoiselle

Contents

Ablan	9
The Abortionist's Horse (A Nightmare)	13
Blue Vase of Ghosts	29
The Ghost (In Two Letters)	53
The Ghost of the Clock	63
The Lady-Of-Shalott House	95
The Minstrel's Tale	109
A Night on the Hill	121
Seeing, Believing	127
The Sky Won't Listen	137
The Squire's Tale	165
Tan	173
Thuvia Made of Mars (Spilt Milk)	177
The Winter Ghosts	195
Yesterday	205
Yesternight	211
Publishing History of the Stories	212
About the Author	214

Ablan

He wandered about the woods and hills by day, and nightly lay against some tree. He tried to eat the edible leaves, or fruits in season. He tried by now not to see how they, his people, moved about in the village below, going on as ever in their usual occupations, and after dark kindling the warm smoky shimmer of their lights. In the past – often at first – unable to help himself, weeping, where now he was obdurately silent, he drifted down into the valley, and in among the village lanes and walls. Into the folds or byres he peered, at the beasts as they chewed, or slumbered. In at the glimmered windows he gazed, watching as families cooked and ate their food, drank beer, sang songs. And after, how they curled to sleep or to join in eager congress. He watched the women feed or rock their babies, the men repair their working gear before the fires. Forever excluded he, cast out by the terrible calamity that had fallen on him, and forever exiled now, able only to stare and sigh, to hang like a moth upon the sill, a raindrop on a pane – ephemeral and of no account. Sometimes, unthinking, one of them might come out into the yard, to urinate, or scan up into the stars. These villagers, encountering him, never saw him, of course not, not even those members of his own family. Once or twice one had, in fact, unknowing, passed – right through him – oh, shock and misery. He could, of course also, not touch them. No single kiss. No loving, yearning, weeping arm extended. He was to them unseen, less than a shadow, less than a fall of dust. Except once, once only. That was with his daughter of fifteen years, his sweet child so soon to be wed, and standing in the open sunlight of the yard she had looked up and, with no warning, seen him. She the only one ever to do so, since death had sliced him from them. But though instantly he held out his hands, begging her not to be afraid, she dropped to her knees, sobbing and screaming, till the others came, and took her in, and he heard them promising her, in voices that, now, were to him faint as if heard across a mountain gulf, that she had seen nothing, *nothing*. It was only sorrow at his loss, only a feminine mistake, some cloud reflected on the wall, some waking dream. And after that he stole away. And never again did he venture too close. To make them afraid, after the horror they had already suffered; he would not do it. He loved them still, though never now might he offer love to them. He kept to the woods and hills, lay against some tree. Watched from a distance. Let his tears, that had been an ocean, dry up like a vat of salt.

The plague had come to Ablan's village in the early spring.
    Within three days many were sick, like to die. But there is generally some immunity. On this occasion fate chose whom should be saved and whom destroyed with an extraordinary and prickly pettiness, and vile cruelty. In a single night, by fits and starts and fits of utter ending, it ordered which must be slain. And left surviving only what might truly suffer.
    What it did leave then, to bear that harsh and undeservedly unforgiveable punishment, was most select: Only Ablan.
    For he alone had survived. Otherwise his family, his wife, his son, his daughters, otherwise the entire village, obliterated.
    And crawling at last from his bed he found them all, everyone a corpse. Only he lived. He, Ablan. No other. Not even their cattle, their sheep, their dogs. All gone. All gone. When first he, wandering half mad about the woods and hills, glimpsed below the lights smoke up at sunfall, he had run down, shouting and amazed – and found them all, about their usual business. Working and eating and drinking, singing and sleeping and making love.
    But he was no longer one of them. Forever then excluded, an outlaw, dead as death in every way – but – true mockery – for *one* way. For he had lived, and they were ghosts, were ghosts.

He wanders about the woods and hills, he tries to sleep, to eat the leaves. His ocean of weeping has turned to salt. He is alive and alone forever, and so more dead, buried in cold flesh, *more* dead than death; Ablan.

The Abortionist's Horse
(A Nightmare)

Naine bought the house in the country because she thought it would be perfect for her future life.

At this time, her future was the core upon and about which she placed everything. She supposed that was instinctive.

The house was not huge, but interesting. Downstairs there was a large stone kitchen recently modernised, packed with units, drawers, cupboards and a double sink, with room for a washing machine, and incorporating a tall slender fridge and an electric cooker with a copper hood. The kitchen led into a small breakfast room with a bay window view of the back garden, a riot of roses, with one tall oak dominating the small lawn. At the front of the house there was also a narrow room that Naine christened the parlour. Opposite this, oddly, was the bathroom, again very modern, with a turquoise suite she would never have chosen but quite liked. Up the narrow stair there were a big linen cupboard, and three rooms, the largest of which was to be Naine's bedroom, with white curtains blowing in fresh summer winds. The two smaller rooms were of almost equal size. One would be her library and workroom. The third room also would come to have a use. It, like the larger bedroom and the parlour, faced to the front, over the lane. But there was never much, if any, traffic on the lane, which no longer led down into the village.

A housing estate had closed the lane thirty years before, but it was half a mile from the house. The village was one mile away. Now you reached it by walking a shady path that ran away behind the garden and down through the fields. A hedgerow-bordered walk, nice in any season.

The light struck Naine, spring light first, and almost

summer light now, and the smells of honeysuckle and cow parsley from the lane, the garden roses, the occasional faint hint of hay and herbivorous manure blowing up the fields.

You could just hear the now and then soft rush of cars on the main road that bypassed the village. And church bells all day Sunday, sounding drowned like the ones in sunken Lyonesse.

Her Uncle Robert's death had given Naine the means for this venture. She had only slightly known him, a stiff memory of a red-brown August man handing her a lolly when she was five, or sitting on a train with the rest of the family when she was about thirteen, staring out of the window, looking sad at a bereavement.

The money was a surprise. Evidently he had had no one else he wanted to give it to.

The night of the day when she learned about her legacy there was a party to launch the book Naine had been illustrating. She had not meant to go, but, keyed up by such sudden fortune, had after all put on a red dress, and taken a taxi to the wine bar. She was high before she even entered, and five white wines completed her elevation. So, in that way, Uncle Robert's bequest was also responsible for what happened next.

At twenty-seven, Naine had slept with only two men.

One had been her boyfriend at twenty-one, taken her virginity, stayed her lover for two years. The second was a relationship she had formed in Sweden for one month. In fact, they had slept together more regularly, almost every night, where with the first man she had only gone to bed with him once or twice a week, so reticent had been their competing schedules. In neither case had Naine felt very much, beyond a slight embarrassment and desire for the act to be satisfactorily over, like a test. She had read enough to pretend, she thought adequately, although her first lover had sadly said, as he left her for ever to go to Leeds, "You're such a cool one." The Swede had apparently believed her sobs and cries. She knew,

The Abortionist's Horse (A Nightmare)

but only from masturbation, that orgasm existed. She had a strange, infallible fantasy, which always worked for her when alone, although never when with a man. She imagined lying in a darkened room, her eyes shut, and that some presence stole towards her. She never knew what it was, but as it came closer and closer, so did she, until, at the expected first touch, climax swept through her end to end.

At the party was a handsome brash young man, who wanted to take Naine to dinner. Drunk, elevated, she accepted. They ended up at his flat in Fulham, and here she allowed him to have sex with her, rewarding his varied and enthusiastic scenario with the usual false sobs and low cries. Perhaps he did not believe in them, or was only a creature of one nights, for she never heard from him or saw him again. This was no loss.

However, six weeks later, she decided she had better see a doctor. In the past her methods of contraception had been irregular, and nothing had ever occurred. It seemed to her, nonsensically but instinctively, that her lack of participation in the act removed any chance of pregnancy. This time, though, the spell had not worked.

Abortions were just legally coming into regular use. For a moment Naine considered having one. But, while believing solidly in any woman's right to have an unwanted foetus removed from her womb, Naine found she did not like the idea when applied to her own body.

Gradually, over the next month, she discovered that she began to think intensely about what was inside her, not as a thing, but as a child. She found herself speaking to it, silently, or even aloud. Sometimes she was even tempted to sing it songs and rhymes, especially those she had liked when small – Here We Go Round the Mulberry Bush, and Ride a Cockhorse to Banbury Cross. Absurd. Innocent. She was amused and tolerant of herself.

Presently she was sure that the new life belonged to her, or at least that she was its sponsor. With this in mind, she set about finding a house in the country where the child might be brought up away from the raucous city of its conception. The house by the lane looked so pretty at once, the cow parsley and docks standing high, the sunlight drifting on a pink rose classically at the door. When she learned there was the new hospital only two miles away in Spaleby, and besides a telephone point in the bedroom for the pre-ordained four-in-the-morning call for an ambulance, Naine took the house. And as she stepped, its owner, in over the threshold, a wave of delight enveloped her, like the clear, spotted sunshine through the leaves.

As Naine walked up to the bus-stop by the main road, she was thinking about what a friend had said to her over the phone, the previous night. "You talk as if it didn't have a father." This had only come to Naine hours afterwards. That is, its import. For it was true. Biology aside, the child was solely hers, and already Naine had begun to speak of it as feminine.

She realised friends had called her less and less, during the fortnight she had been here. In the beginning their main interest had seemed to be if she was feeling 'horribly' ill – she never was. Also how she had 'covered' herself. Naine had put on her dead mother's wedding ring, which was a little loose, and given the impression she and a husband were separated.

Once the friends knew she was neither constantly spewing nor being witch-hunted as a wanton, they drew off. Really, were they her friends anyway? She had always tended to be solitary, and in London had gone out perhaps one night in thirty, and that probably reluctantly. She enjoyed her work, music, reading, even simply sitting in front of the TV, thinking about other things.

The bus-stop had so far been deserted when Naine twice came to it about three, for the 3.15 bus to Spaleby. Today, in time for the 1.15 bus, she saw a woman was already waiting there. She was quite an ordinary woman, bundled in a shabby coat, maybe sixty, cheerful and nosy. She turned at once to Naine.

"Hallo, dear. You've timed it just right."

Naine smiled. She wondered if the woman could see the child, faintly curved under the loose cotton dress. The bulge was very small.

"You're in Number 23, aren't you?" asked the woman.

"Oh... yes. I am."

"Thought so. Yes. I saw you the other day, hanging your washing out, as I were going down the lane."

Naine had a vague recollection of occasional travellers using the lane, on foot, between the stands of juicy plants and overhanging trees. Either they were going to the estate, or, climbing over the style, making off across the land in the opposite direction, where there were three farms, and what was still locally termed the Big House, a small, derelict and woebegone manor.

"Miss your hubby, I expect," said the woman.

Naine smiled once more. Of course she did, normal woman that she was; yes.

"Never mind. Like a lot of the women when I was a girl. The men had to go to Spaleby, didn't come back except on the Sunday. There was houses all up the lane then. Twenty-seven in all, there was. Knocked down. There's the pity. Just Number 23 left. And then modernised. My, I can remember when there wasn't even running water at 23. But you'll have all the mod cons now, I expect."

"Yes, thank you."

"I expect you've done a thing or two to the house. I shouldn't wonder if you have."

Naine sensed distinctly the nosy cheerful woman would love to come in and look at Number 23, and she, Naine, would now have to be on guard, when the doorbell rang. "I haven't done much."

"Just wait till hubby gets home. Shelves and I don't know what-all."

Naine smiled, smiled, and wished the bus would arrive. But she would anticipate Naine would sit with her, no doubt. Some excuse would have to be found. Or the guts to be rude and simply choose another seat.

Two cars went by, going too fast, were gone.

"Now the lane used to go right through to the village, in them days. There wasn't no high road here, neither. You used to hear the girls mornings, going out at four on the dot, to get to the Big House. Those that didn't live in. But the Missus didn't encourage it. She was that strict. Had to be. Then, there was always old Alice Barterlowe." The woman gave a sharp, sniggering laugh. It was an awful laugh, somehow obscene. And her eyes glittered with malice. Did Naine imagine it – she tried to decide afterwards – those eyes glittering on her belly as the laugh died down. At the time Naine felt compelled to say, "Alice Barterlowe? Who was that?" It was less the cowardly compulsion to be polite than a desire to clear the laugh from the air.

"Who was *she*? Well that's funny, dear. She was a real character hereabouts. When I was a nipper, that were. A real character, old Alice."

"Really."

"Oh my. She kept herself to herself, did old Alice. But everyone knew her. Dressed like a man, an old labouring man, and rode astride. But no one said a word. You could hear her, coming down that lane, always at midnight. That was her hour. The hoofs on the lane, and you didn't look out. There goes Alice, my sister said once, when we'd been woke up, and then she put her hand over her mouth, like she shouldn't have said it. Nor she shouldn't. No one was meant to know, you see. But handy for some."

This sinister and illogical dialogue ended. The woman closed her mouth as tight as if zippered. And, before Naine could question her further – or not, perhaps – the green bus came chugging along the road.

"Old Alice Barterlowe. Oh my goodness yes. I can remember my gran telling me about her. If it was true."

The Abortionist's Horse (A Nightmare)

It was five days later, and the chatty girl in the village shop was helping Naine load her bag with one loaf, one cabbage, four apples and a pound of sausages.

"Who was she?"

"Oh, an old les. But open about it as you like. She had a lady-friend lived with her. But she died. Alice used to dress up just like the men, and she rode this old mare. Couldn't miss her, gran said, but then you didn't often see her. You *heard* her go by."

"At midnight."

"Midnight, that's it."

"Why? Where was she going?"

"To see to the girls."

"I'm sorry?"

"Girls up the duff, like."

"You mean... you mean pregnant?"

"She was an abortionist, was Alice."

Naine had only felt sick once, a week after she had moved in. Sitting with her feet up for half an hour had taken it right off. Now she felt as if someone was trying to push her stomach up through her mouth. She retched silently, as the chatty girl, missing it, rummaged through her till.

I will *not* be sick.

I *won't*.

The nausea sank down like an angry sea, leaving her pale as the now hideous, unforgiveable slab of cheese on the counter.

"Here you are. Three pound change. Yes, old Alice, and that old horse. Half dead it looked, said my gran, but went on for years. And old les Alice was filthy. And this dirty old bag slung on the saddle. But she kept her hands clean as a whistle. And her stuff. There wasn't one girl she seen to come to harm."

"You mean – it didn't work."

"Oh it *worked*. It worked all right. They all got rid of them as wanted to, that Alice saw to. She was reliable. And not one of them got sick. A clean healthy miscarriage. Though my gran said, not one ever got in the family way after. Not even if she could by then. Not once Alice had seen to her."

On the homeward shady path between the hedges and fields, Naine went to the side and threw up easily and quickly among the clover. It was the sausages, she thought, and getting in, threw them away, dousing the bin after with TCP.

Ride a cock-horse to Banbury Cross,
  To see a fine lady upon a white horse–

The rhyme went round in Naine's head as she lay sleepily, waking at five in the summer morning. The light had come, and patched beautifully through her beautiful butterfly-white curtains. On a white horse, on a white horse –

And something sour was sitting waiting, invisible, unknowable, not really there.

Old Alice Barterlowe.

Well, she had done some good, surely. Poor little village girls in the days before the Pill, led on by men who wouldn't marry them, and the poor scullery maids seduced at the Big House by some snobby male relative of the strict Missus. What choice did they have but those clean strong probing fingers, the shrill hot-cold pain, the flush of blood –

Naine sat up. Don't think of it.

Ride a cock-horse, clip clop. Clip clop.

And poor old Alice, laughed at and feared, an ugly old lesbian whose lover had died. Poor old Alice, whose abortions always worked. Riding astride her ruinous old mare.

Down the lane. Midnight. Clip clop. Clip clop.

Stop it.

"I'll get up, and we'll have some tea," said Naine aloud to her daughter, curled soft and safe within her.

But in the end she could not drink the tea and threw it away. A black cloud hung over the fields, and rain fell like galloping.

When Naine phoned her friends now, they could never stay very long. One had a complex dinner on and guests coming.

The Abortionist's Horse (A Nightmare)

One had to meet a boyfriend. One had an ear infection and talking on the phone made her dizzy. They all said Naine sounded tired. Was there a sort of glee in their voices? Serve her right.

Not like them. If she *wanted* to get pregnant and make herself ill and mess up her life –

Naine sat in the rocker, rocking gently, talking and singing to her child. As she did so she ran her hands over and over along the hard small swelling. I feel like a smooth, ripening melon.

"There's a hole in my bucket, dear daughter, dear daughter..."

Naine, dozing. The sun so warm. The smell of honeysuckle. Sounds of bees. The funny nursery rhyme tapping at the brain's back, clip *clop*, clip *clop*.

Naine was dreaming. She was on the Tube in London, and it was terribly hot, and the train kept stopping, there in the dark tunnels. Everyone complained, and a man with a newspaper kept saying, "It's a fly. A fly's got in."

Naine knew she was going to be terribly late, although she was not sure for what, and this made it much worse. If only the train would come into the station, then she might have time to recollect.

"I tell you there's a fly!" the man shouted in her face.

"Then do it up," said Naine, arrogantly.

She woke, her heart racing, sweat streaming down her, soaking her cotton nightdress.

Thank God it was over, and she was here, and everything was all right. Naine sat up, and pushed her pillows into a mound she could lean against.

Through the cool white curtains, a white half moon was silkily shining. A soft rustle came from the trees as the lightest of calm night breezes passed over and over, visiting the leaves.

Naine reflected, as one sometimes does, on the power of the silliest dreams to cause panic. On its Freudian symbols –

tunnels, trains, *flies*.

She stroked her belly. "Did I disturb you, darling? It's all right now." She drank some water, and softly sang, without thinking, what was tapping there in her brain, "Clip *clop*, clip *clop*. Clip *clop*, clip *clop*. Here comes the abortionist's *horse*." Then she was rigid. "Oh Christ." She got out of bed and stood in the middle of the floor. "Christ, Christ."

And then she was turning her head. It was midnight.

She could see the clock. She had woken at just the proper hour. Alice Barterlowe's hour.

Clip *clop*, clip *clop*...

The lane, but for the breeze, was utterly silent. Up on the main road, came a gasp of speed as one of the rare nocturnal cars spun by. Across the fields, sometimes, an owl might call. But not tonight. Tonight there was no true sound at all. And certainly not – *that* sound.

All she had to do now, like a scared child, was to be brave enough to go to the window, pull back the curtain a little, and look out. There would be nothing there. Nothing at all.

It took her some minutes to be brave enough. Then, as she pulled back the curtain, she felt a hot-cold stinging pass all through her, like an electric shock. But it was only her stupid and irrational night-fear. Nothing at all was in the lane, as she had known nothing at all would be. Only the fronds of growing things, ragged and prehistoric under the moon, and the tall trees clung with shadows.

Past all the houses Alice had ridden on the slow old wreck of the horse, down the lane, and through the village.

To a particular cottage, to a hidden room. In the dark, the relentless hands, the muffled cries, the sobs. And later, the black gushing away that had been a life.

Why did she do it? To get back at men? Was it only her compassion for her own beleaguered sex, in those days when women were more inferior than, supposedly, during the days of Naine?

Go away, Alice. Your time is over.

The Abortionist's Horse (A Nightmare)

It was so silent, in the lane.
Clip *clop*, clip *clop*, clip *clop*, clip *clop*.
Here comes...
Naine went downstairs to the bathroom. She felt better after she had been sick. She took a jug of water and her portable radio back upstairs. A night station played her the Beatles, Pink Floyd, and even an aria by Puccini, until she fell asleep, curled tight, holding her child to her, hard, against the filmy night.

The doctor in Spaleby was pleased with Naine. He told her she was doing wonderfully, but seemed a bit tired. She must remember not to do too much. When they were seated again, he said, sympathetically, "I suppose there isn't any chance of that husband of yours turning up?"

Naine realised with a slight jolt she had been convincing enough to convince even the doctor.

"No. I don't think so."

"Some men," he said. He looked exasperated. Then he cheered up. "Never mind. You've got the best thing there."

When she was walking to the town bus-stop, Naine felt weary and heavy, for the first time. The heat seemed oppressive, and the seat for the stop was tormentingly arranged in clear burning yellow light. Two fat women already sat there, and made way for her grudgingly. She was always afraid at this point of meeting the awful, cheery, nosy woman. Because of the awful woman, Naine no longer pegged out washing, and had kept the postman waiting on her doorstep twice, while she peered at him from an upstairs room, to be sure.

Somehow, to see the awful woman again would be just too much. She might start talking about Alice Barterlowe. Naine was sure that her child, in its fifth month, was generally visible by now. That would set the awful woman off, probably. *No use for old Alice, then*. No. No.

When the bus came, the journey seemed to last for a year, although it took less than half an hour. All the stops, and at every stop, some woman with a bag. And these women, though not the awful woman, might still sit beside her, might say, "Oh, you're at Number 23 in the lane. The lane where the abortionist rode by at midnight on her nag."

Exhausted, Naine walked down from the main road. She made herself a jug of barley water and sipped a glass on the shady side of her garden. The grass had gone wild, was full of daisies, dandelions, nettles, purple sage, and butterflies.

"I'm so happy here. It's so perfect. It's what we want. I mustn't be so silly, must I?" But neither must she ever speak her fear aloud to her child. Of all the things she could tell the child – not this, never this.

And round and round in her head, the idiotic rhyme, compounded of others that had gone wrong...

Clip *clop*, clip *clop*.

She must have been courageous. Alice. To live as she did, and do what she did. Especially then. It took courage now. Naine could recall the two girls caught kissing at school, and the ridiculous to-do there had been. Did they *know* what they were *doing*? Dirty, nasty. They had been shunned, and only forgiven when one confessed to pretending the other was a boy. They were *practicing* for men. For their proper female function and role.

Naine, of course, was properly fulfilling both. Naine must like men, obviously. Look at her condition. It was her husband who was in the wrong. She had been faithful, loving, admiring, aroused, orgasmic, conceptive, productive. But he had run off. Oh yes, Naine was absolutely fine.

She did not want any dinner, or supper. She would have to economise, stop buying all this food she repeatedly had to throw away.

But then, she had to eat, for the sake of the child.

"I will, tomorrow, darling. Your mother won't be so silly tomorrow."

She had told the doctor she could not sleep, made the mistake of saying, "I keep listening –"

But he was ahead of her, thank God. "The pressure on the stomach and lungs can be a nuisance, I'm afraid. Ask nurse to give you a leaflet. And you've only moved out here recently. I know, these noisy country nights. Foxes, badgers rustling about. Whoever said the country was quiet was mad. It took me six months to get used to it." He added that sleeping pills were not really what he would advise. "Try cutting down on tea and coffee after 5 pm, some herbal infusion maybe, and honey." And so on.

After the non-event of dinner, Naine watched her black and white eighteen inch TV until the close down. Then she went next door and had a bath.

She had never been quite happy with the bathroom downstairs. It could be grim later, when she was even heavier, lumbering up and down with bladder pressure, to pee. Maybe when things were settled anyway, she could move the bathroom upstairs, put the work-room here.

The child's room, the room the child would have; she had been going to paint that, and she ought to do so.

Blue and pink were irrelevant. A sort of buttermilk colour would be ideal. Pale curtains like her own. And both rooms facing onto the lane. It would not matter about the lane, then. By then, Naine would laugh at it, but not the way the awful woman had laughed.

Clip *clop*. Clip *clop*.

After the bath, bed. Sitting up. Reading a novel, the same line over and over, or half a page, which was like reading something in ancient Greek. And the silence. The silence waiting for the sound.

Clip *clop*.

Turn on the radio. Bad reception sometimes. Crackling. Love songs. Songs of loss. All the lovely normal women weeping for lost men, and wanting them back at any cost.

At last, eyes burning, lying down. We'll go to sleep now.

But not. The silence, between the notes of the radio. A car. A fox. The owl. The wind. Waiting...

Clip *clop*, clip *clop*.

It was the horse she couldn't bear. It was the horse she saw. Not old Alice in her dirty labourer's clothes, with her scrubbed hands and white nails. The horse. The horse whose hoofs were the sound that said, Here comes Alice, Alice on her horse.

Old horse. Try to feel sorry for the poor old horse, as try to feel proud of courageous Alice. But no, the horse's face was long and haggard, with rusty drooping eyes, yellow, broken, blunt teeth, dribbling, unkempt. Not a sad face. An evil face. The pale horse of death.

"I'm sorry I can't sleep, baby. You sleep. You sleep and I'll sing you a lullaby. Hush-a-bye, hush-a-bye."

But the words are wrong. The words are about the white pale horse. The night-mare. The nag with the fine lady, the old lesbian. Clippity-clop –

Clip *clop* clip *clop*.

Clip *clop* clip *clop*.

It was coming up in her, up from her stomach, her throat, like sick. She couldn't hold it in.

"Clip clop clip clop clip clop clip clop here comes the abortionist's horse!"

And then she laughed the evil laugh, and she knew how it had trundled and limped down the lane, its hoofs clipping and clicking, carrying death to the unborn through the mid of night.

"It's my work that's the problem. I didn't realise it would be so awkward." She was explaining to the estate agent, who sat looking at her as if trying to fathom the secret. "I'll just have to sell up and get back to London. It really is a nuisance."

"Well, Mrs Robert... well, we'll see what we can do."

As Naine again sat on the hot seat waiting for the bus, she thought of the train journey to London, of having nowhere to go. She had tried her friends, tentatively, to see if she could bivouac a day or two. One had not answered at all. One cut her short with a tale of personal problems. You could never intrude. One said she was so sorry, but she had decorators in.

The Abortionist's Horse (A Nightmare)

This last sounded like a lie, but probably was true. In any case, it would have to be a hotel, and the furniture would have to be stored. And then, flat-hunting, five months gone, in the deep, smoky city heat. The house had been affordable down here. But London prices would allow her little scope.

It doesn't matter. I can find somewhere better after you're born. But for now. For now.

She knew she was a fool, had perhaps gone a bit crazy as they said women did during pregnancy and the menopause. Even the kind doctor, when she had vaguely confessed to irrational anxieties, said jokingly, "I'm afraid that can be par for the course. Hormones."

To leave the house – *her* house – how she had loved it. But now. Not now.

No one came to look at the house, however. When she phoned the agent, they were evasive. It was a long way out unless you liked walking or had a car. And there had been a threat of the bus service being cut.

Day by day.

Night by night.

Over and over.

Its face.

The horse.

She was dreaming again, but even unconscious, she recognised the dream. It was delicious. So long since she had felt the tingling. This promise of pleasure. Her sexual fantasy.

She was in the darkened room. Everything was still. Yet someone approached, unseen.

They glided, behind dim floating curtains. The faint whisper of movement. And at every sound, her anticipation was increasing. In the heart of her loins, a building marvellous tension.

Yes, yes. Oh come to me.

Naine, sleeping, sensed the drawing close. And now her groin thrummed, drum-taut. Waiting...

The shadow was there. It leaned towards her.

As her pulses escalated to their final pitch, she heard its ill-shod metal feet on the floor. A leaden midnight fell through her body and her blood was cold.

Its long horse face, primal, pathetic and cruel. The broken teeth. The rusty, rust-dripping half-blind eyes. It hung over her like a cloud, and she smelled its smell, hay and manure, stone and iron, old rain, ruinous silence, crying and sobbing, and the stink of pain and blame and bones.

The horse. It was here. It breathed into her face.

Naine woke, and the night was empty, noiseless, and then she felt the trapped and stifled pleasure, which had become a knot of spikes, and stumbling, half falling down the stairs, to the inconvenient lower bathroom, she left a trail of blood.

Here, under the harsh electric light, vomiting in the bath, heaving out to the lavatory between her thighs the reason, the light, the life of her life, in foam and agony and a gush of scarlet, Naine wept and giggled, choking on her horror. And all the while knowing, she had nothing to dread, would heal very well, as all Alice's girls did. Knowing, like all Alice's girls, she would never again conceive a child.

Blue Vase of Ghosts

1. Subyrus, the Magician

Above, the evening sky; dark blue, transparent and raining stars. Below, the evening-coloured land, also blue to the depths of its hills, its river-carven valley, blue to its horizon, where a dusting of gold freckles revealed the lights of the city of Vaim.

Between, a bare hillside with two objects on it: a curious stone pavilion and a frightened man.

The cause of the man's fear, evidently, was the pavilion, or what it signified. Nevertheless, he had advanced to the open door and was peering inside.

The entire landscape had assumed the romantic air of faint menace that attends twilight, all outlines darkening and melting in the mysterious smoke of dusk. The pavilion appeared no more sinister than everything else. About eight feet in height, with a flat roof set on five walls of rough-hewn slabs, its only truly occult area lay over the square step and through the square door mouth – a matched square of black shadow.

Until: "I seek the Magician-Lord Subyrus," the frightened man exclaimed aloud, and the black shadow vanished in an ominous brazen glare.

The man gasped. Not so much in fear, as in uneasy recognition of something expected. Nor did he cry out, turn to run, or fall on his knees when, in the middle of the glare, there stood an unnatural figure. It was a great toad, large as a dog and made of brass, which parted its jaws with a creaking of metal hinges, and asked: "*Who* seeks Subyrus, Master of the Ten Mechanicae?"

"My name is not important," quavered the man. "My mission is. Lord Subyrus is interested in purchasing rarities of magic. I bring him one."

Galaxies glinted and wheeled in bulbous amphibian eyes.

"Very well," the toad said. "My maker hears. You are invited in. Enter."

At which the whole floor of the pavilion rushed upwards, with the monster squatting impassively atop it. Revealed beneath was a sort of metal cage, big enough to contain a man. Into this cage all visitors must step, and the frightened visitor knew as much.

Just as he had known of the hill, the pavilion, the glare of unseen lamps and the horrendous brazen guardian. For down the trade roads and throughout the river ports of Vaim, word of these wonders had spread, along with the news that Subyrus, Master of the Ten Mechanicae, would buy with gold objects of sorcery – providing they were fabulous, bizarre and, preferably, unique.

The visitor entered the cage, which was the second of the Ten Mechanicae (the toad being the first).The cage instantly plunged into the hollow hill.

His entrails seemingly left plastered to the pavilion roof by the rapid descent, this visitor clutched to himself the leather satchel he had brought, and thought alternately of riches and death.

Subyrus sat in a chair of green quartz in a hall hung with drapes the colours of charred roses and black panthers. A clear pink fire burned on the wide hearth that gave off the slight persuasive scent of strawberries. Subyrus studied the fire quietly with deep-lidded dark eyes. He had the face of a beautiful skull, long hands and a long leopardine body to concur with that image. The robe of murky murderous crimson threw into exotic relief his luminous and unblemished pallor, and the strange dull bronze of his long hair that seemed carved rather than combed.

When the cage dashed down into the hall and bounced on its cushioned buffers, throwing the occupant all awry, Subyrus looked up, unsmiling. He regarded the man who staggered from the cage clutching a satchel, with none of the cruel arid expressions or gestures the man had obviously anticipated.

Subyrus's regard was compounded of pity, a vague inquiry, an intense drugged boredom.

It was, if anything, worse than sadism and savagery.

A melodramatic laugh and a glimpse of wolf-fangs would have been somehow preferable to those opaque and disenchanted eyes.

"Well?" Subyrus said. Less a question than a plea – *Oh, for the love of the gods, interest me in something.* The plea of a man (if he were that alone) to whom other men were insects, and their deeds pages of a book to be turned and turned in the vain hope of a quickening.

The man with the satchel quailed.

"Magician-Lord – I had heard – you wished marvels to be brought to you that you might...acquire them?"

Subyrus sighed.

"You heard correctly. What then have you brought?"

"In this satchel, lordly one – something beyond –"

"Beyond what?" Subyrus's sombre eyes widened, but only with disbelief at the tedium this salesman was causing him. "Beyond my wildest dreamings, perhaps you meant say? I have no wild dreamings. I should welcome them."

In a panic, the man with the satchel blurted something. The sort of overplay he might have used on an ordinary customer; it had become a habit with him to attempt startlement in order to gain the upper hand. But not here, where he should have left well alone.

"What did you say?" Subyrus asked.

"I said – I said –"

"Yes?"

"That the Lady Lunaria of Vaim – was wild dream enough."

Now the satchel-man stood transfixed at his own idiocy, his very bones knocking together in wretched fright. Indeed, Subyrus had lost his mask of boredom, but it had been replaced merely by an appalling contempt.

"Have I become a laughing stock in Vaim?"

The query was idle, mild. Suddenly the man with the satchel realised the contempt of the magician was self-directed. The man slumped and answered, truthfully: "No one would dare laugh, Magician-Lord, at anything of yours. The length of the river, men pale at your name. But the other thing – you can hardly blame them for envying you the Lady Lunaria." He glanced up. Had he said the right words, at last? The magician did not respond. The frightened satchel-man had space to brood on the story then current in the city, that the Master of the Ten Mechanicae had taken for his mistress the most famous whore this side of the northern ocean, and that Lunaria Vaimian ruled Subyrus as if he were a toothless lion, ordering him to this and that, demanding costly gifts, setting him errands, and even in the matter of the bedchamber, herself saying when. Some claimed the story was an invention of Lunaria's, a dangerous game she played with Subyrus's reputation. Others said that Subyrus himself had sent the fancy abroad to see if any dared mock him, so he might cut them down with sorcery in some vicious and perverse fashion.

But the satchel-man had come off the mountain roads to Vaim. A stranger, he had never seen Lunaria for himself, nor, till tonight, the magician-lord.

"Well?" Subyrus said drowsily.

The satchel-man jumped in his skin.

"I suggest," Subyrus said, "you show me this rare treasure beyond wild dreamings. You may mention its origin and how you came by it. You may state its ability, if any, and demonstrate. You may then name your price. But, I beg you, no more sales patter."

Shivering, the satchel-man undid the clasps and drew from the leather a padded bag. From the bag he produced a velvet box. In the box he revealed a sapphire glimmer wrapped in feathers. The feathers drifted to the floor as he lifted out a vase of blue crystal, about a foot in length, elongated of neck, with a broad base of oddly alternating swelling and tapering design. The castellated lip was sealed by a stopper that appeared to be a single rose-opal.

Prudently silent, and holding the vase before him like a talisman, the visitor approached Subyrus's chair.

"Charming," Subyrus said. "But what does it do?"

"My lord," the satchel-man whispered, "my lord – I can simply recount what it is *supposed* to have done – and to do. I myself have not the skill to test it."

"Then you must tell me immediately how you came by it. Look at me," Subyrus added. His voice was all at once no longer indolent but cool and terrible. Unwilling, but without choice, the satchel-man raised his head. Subyrus was turning a great black ring, round and round, on his finger. At first it was like a black snake darting in and out, then like a black eye, opening and closing.

Subyrus sighed again, depressed at the ease with which most human resistance could be overcome.

"Speak now."

The satchel-man dutifully began.

Mesmerised by the black ring, he spoke honestly, without either embroidery or omission.

2. The Satchel-Man's Tale

An itinerant scavenger by trade, the satchel-man had happened on a remote town of the far north, and learned of a freakish enterprise taking place in the vicinity. The tomb of an ancient king had been located in the heart of one of the tall iron-blue crags that towered above the town. Scholars of the town, fascinated by the tomb's antiquity, had hired gangs of workmen to break into the inner chamber and prise off the lid of the sarcophagus. At this event, the satchel-man was a lurking bystander. He had made up to several of the scholars in the hope of some arcane jewel dropping into his paws. But in the end, all that had been uncovered were dust, stench, decay and some brown grinning bones – clutched in the digits of which was a vase of blue crystal stoppered with a rose-opal.

The find being solitary, the scholars were obliged to offer it to the town's Tyrant.

He graciously accepted the vase, attempted to pull out the opal stopper; failed, attempted to smash the vase in order to release the stopper; failed, ordered various pounding devices to crush the vase – which also failed, called for one of the scholars and demanded he investigate the nature of the vase forthwith. This scholar, who had leanings in the sorcerous direction, had also become the host of the parasitic satchel-man. The satchel-man had spun some yarn of ill luck, which the scholar, an unworldly intellectual, credited.

So the satchel-man was informed as to the scholar's magical assaults on the vase. Not that the satchel-man actually attended the rituals first hand (as, but for the mesmerism, he would have assured Subyrus he had). Yet he was advised of them over supper, when the fraught scholar complained of his unsuccess. Then late one night, as the satchel-man sprawled on a couch with his host's brandy pitcher, a fearsome yell echoed through the house. A second or so later, pale as steamed fish, the scholar stumbled into the room, and collapsed whimpering on the ground.

The satchel-man gallantly revived the scholar with some of his own brandy. The scholar spoke.

"It is sorcery of the Brink, the Abyss. More lethal than the sword, and more dreadful. In the hands of a Power, what mischief could it not encompass? What mischief it *has* encompassed."

"Have a little more brandy," said the satchel-man, torn between curiosity, avarice and nerves. "Say more."

The scholar drank deep, grew sozzled, and elaborated in such a way that the hairs bristled on the satchel-man's unclean neck.

Searching an antique book, the scholar had discovered an unusual spell of Opening. This he had performed, and the rose-opal had jumped free of the mouth of the vase. Such a whirling had then occurred inside it that the scholar had become alarmed. The crystal seemed full of milk on the boil and milky lather foamed in the opening of the castellated mouth. In consternation, the scholar had given vent to numerous rhetorical questions, such as: "What shall I do?" and "What in the world does this bubbling portend?" Finally he voiced a rhetorical question that utilised the name of the ancient king: "What can King So-and-so have performed with such an artefact?"

Rhetorical questions do not expect answers. But to this question an answer came.

No sooner was the king's name uttered than the frothing in the vase erupted outwards. A strand of this froth, proceeding higher than the rest from the vase's mouth, gradually solidified. Within the space of half a minute, there balanced in the atmosphere above the vase, deadly white but perfectly formed, the foot-high figure of a man, lavishly bearded and elaborately clad, a barbaric diadem on his head. With a minute sneer, this figure addressed the scholar:

"Normally, further ritual with greater accuracy is required. But since I was the last to enter, and since I have been within a mere four centuries, I respond to my name. Well, what do you wish, O absurd and gigantic fool?"

A dialogue then ensued which had to do with the scholar's astonishment and disbelief, and the white midget king's utter irritation at, and scorn of, the scholar.

In the course of this dialogue, however, the nature of the vase was specified.

A magician had made it, though when and how was unsure. Its purpose was original, providing the correct magic had been activated by rite and incantation. That done, whoever might die – or whoever might be slain – in the close neighbourhood of the vase, their soul would be sucked into the crystal and imprisoned there till the ending of time, or at least time as mortal men know it. Since its creation, countless magicians, and others who had learned the relevant sorcery, had used the vase in this way, catching inside it the souls, or ghosts, of enemies, lovers and kindred for personal solace or entertainment. It might be reckoned (the king casually told the scholar) that seven thousand souls now inhabited the core of the vase. ("How is there room for so many?" the scholar cried. The king laughed. "I am not bound to answer questions. Therefore, I will do no more than assure you that room there is, and to spare.") It appeared that whoever could name the vase-trapped ghosts by their exact appellations, might call them forth.

They might then reply to interrogation – but only if the fancy took them to do so.

The scholar, overwhelmed, dithered. At length the miniature being demanded leave to return into the vase, which the scholar had weakly granted. He had then flown downstairs to seek comfort from the satchel-man.

The satchel-man was not comforting. He was insistent. The scholar must summon the king's ghost up once again. Positively, the king would be able to tell them where the hoards of his treasure had been buried, for all kings left treasure hoards at death, if not in their tombs, then in some other spot. Was the scholar not a magus? He must recall the ghost and somehow coerce it into malleability, thereby unearthing incredible secrets of lore and (better) cash.

The scholar, convinced by the satchel-man's persistence and the dregs of the brandy, eventually resummoned the king's ghost. Nothing happened. The scholar and the satchel-man strenuously reiterated the summons. Still nothing. It seemed the ghost had been right in hinting that the ritual was important. He had obeyed on the first occasion because his had been the last and newest soul in the vase, but he had no need to obey further without proper incentive.

Then the scholar fell to philosophising and the satchel-man fell to cursing him. Presently the scholar turned the satchel-man out of his house. That night, while the scholar snored in brandy-pickled slumber, the satchel-man regained entry and stole the vase. It was not his first robbery, and his exit was swift from practice.

Thereafter he wandered, endeavouring to locate a mage who knew the correct magic to name, draw forth and browbeat the ghosts in the vase. Or even merely to draw out the rose-opal stopper with which the scholar had inconsiderately recorked it.

Months passed with the mission unaccomplished, and despair set in. Until the satchel-man caught word of the Magician-Lord Subyrus.

To begin with, the satchel-man may have indulged in a dream of enlisting Subyrus's aid, but rumour dissuaded him from this notion. In the long run, it seemed safer to sell the vase outright and be rid of the profitless item. If any mage alive could deal with the thing it was the Master of the Ten Mechanicae. And somehow the salesman did not think Subyrus would share his knowledge. To accept payment in gold seemed the wisest course.

The satchel-man came to himself and saw the fire on the wide hearth had changed. It was green now, and perfumed with apples. The fire must be the third of the Mechanicae.

Subyrus had not changed. Not at all.

"And your price?" he gently murmured. His eyes were nearly shut.

"Considering the treasure I forego in giving up the vase to your lordship–" The satchel-man meant to sound bold, succeeded in a whining tone.

"And considering you will never reach that treasure, as you have no power over the vase yourself," Subyrus amended, and shut his eyes totally from weariness.

"Seven thousand vaimii," stated the satchel-man querulously. "One for each of the seven thousand ghosts in the vase."

Subyrus's lids lifted. He stared at the satchel-man and the satchel-man felt his joints loosen in horror. Then Subyrus smiled. It was the smile of an old, old man, dying of ennui, his mood lightened for a split second by the antics of a beetle on the wall.

"That seems," said Subyrus, "quite reasonable."

One hand moved lazily and the fourth of the Mechanicae manifested itself; it was a brazen chest which sprang from between the charred-rose draperies. Subyrus spoke to the chest, a compartment shot out and deposited a paralysing quantity of gold coins on the rugs at the satchel-man's feet.

"Seven thousand vaimii," Subyrus said. "Count them."

"My lord, I would not suppose–"

"Count them," repeated the magician, without emphasis.

Anxious not to offend, the satchel-man did as he was bid.

He was not a particularly far-sighted man. He did not realise how long it would take him.

A little over an hour later, fingers numb, eyes watering and spine unpleasantly locked, he slunk into the mechanical cage and was borne back to the surface. This time, his guts were left plastered to the lowermost floor of the hollow hill.

Musically clinking, and in terror lest he himself should be robbed, the satchel-man limped hurriedly away through the starry and beautiful night.

3. Proving the Vase

The fire burned warmly black, and smelled of musk and ambergris. This was the aspect of the fire which Subyrus used to recall Lunaria to him. The idea of her threaded his muscles, his very bones, with an elusive excitement, not quite sexual, not quite pleasing, not quite explicable. In this mood, he did not even visualise Lunaria Vaimian as a woman, or as any sort of object. Abstract, her memory possessed him and folded him round with an intoxicating, though distant and scarcely recognisable, agony.

It was quite true that she, of the entire city of Vaim, defied him. She asked him continually for gifts, but she would not accept money or jewels. She wanted the benefits of his status as a magician. So he gave her a rose which endlessly bloomed, gloves that changed colour and material, a ring that could detect the lies of others and whistle thinly, to their discomfort. He collected sorcerous trinkets and bought them for gold, to give to her. In response to these gifts, Lunaria Vaimian admitted Subyrus to her couch. But she also dallied with other men. Twice she had shut her doors to the Master of the Ten Mechanicae. Once, when he had smitten the doors wide, she had said to him: "Do I anger you, lord? Kill me, then. But if you lie with me against my will, I warn you, mighty Subyrus, it will be poor sport."

On various occasions, she had publicly mocked him, struck him in the face, reviled his aptitude both for magic and love. Witnesses had trembled. Subyrus's inaction surprised and misled them.

They reckoned him besotted with a lovely harlot, and wondered at it, that he found her so indispensible he must accept her whims and never rebuke her for them. In fact, Lunaria was indispensible to the Magician-Lord, but not after the general interpretation.

Her skin was like that dark brown spice called cinnamon, her eyes the darker shade of malt. On this sombreness was superimposed a blanching of blonde hair, streaked gold by sunlight and artifice in equal measure. Beautiful she was, but not much more beautiful than several women who had cast themselves at the feet of Subyrus, abject and yielding. Indeed, the entire metropolis and hinterland of Vaim knew and surrendered to him. All-powerful and all-feared and, with women who beheld his handsomeness and guessed at his intellect, all-worshipped. All that, save by Lunaria. Hence, her value. She was the challenge he might otherwise find in no person or sphere. The natural and the supernatural he could control, but not her. She was not abject nor easy. She did not yield. The exacerbation of her defiance quickened him and gave him a purpose, an excuse for his life, in which everything else might be won at a word.

But this self-analysis he concealed from himself with considerable cunning. He experienced only the pangs of her rejection and scorn, and winced as he savoured them like sour wine. Obsessed, he gazed at the vase of blue crystal, and pondered the toys of magic he had given her formerly.

The vase.

The stopper of rose-opal had already been removed by one of the spells of the Forax Foramen, a copy of which ancient book (there were but three copies on earth) was the property of Subyrus. At this spell, written in gold leaf on sheets of black bull's hide, Subyrus had barely glanced. His knowledge was vast and his sorcerous vocabulary extensive. The stopper leapt from the neck of the vase – Subyrus caught it and set it by. Inside the crystal there commenced the foaming and lathering which the scholar had described to the satchel-man.

At Subyrus's other hand lay a second tome. No exact copies of this book existed, for it was the task of each individual mage to compile his own version. The general title of such a compendium being 'Tabulas Mortem, Lists of the Dead'.

From these lists Subyrus had selected seventy names, a hundredth portion of the number of souls said to be trapped in the vase. They were accordingly names of those who had died in peculiar circumstances, and in an aura of shadows, such as might indicate the nearness at that time of the soul-snaring crystal and of someone who could operate its magic.

With each name there obtained attendant rituals of appeasement, summoning and other things that might apply when wishing to contact the dead. All were subtly different from each other, however similar seeming to the uneducated eye.

The fire sank on the hearth now, paled, and began to smell of incense and moist rank soil.

Subyrus had performed the correct ritual and called the first name. He omitted from it the five inflections that would extend the summons beyond the world, since his intent was centred on the trapped ghosts of the vase. He had also discarded the name of the king from whose tomb the vase had been taken. Occult theory suggested that such a spirit, having been recently obedient to an inaccurate summons, (such as the scholar's), could thereby increase its resistance to obeying any other summons for some while after. So the name Subyrus named was a fresh one. Nor, though the ritual was perfect, was it answered.

That soul, then, had never been encaged in the vase. Subyrus erased the name from his selection, and commenced the ritual for a second name.

In Vaim it was midnight, and over the hill above the magician's subculum the configurations of midnight were jewelled out in stars.

Subyrus spoke the nineteenth name.

And was answered.

The moistureless foam-clouds gathered and overspilled the vase. White bubbles and curlicues expanded on the air. From their midst flowed up a slender strand unlike the rest, which proceeded to form a recognisable shape. Presently, a foot-high figurine balanced on the air, just over the castellated lip of the vase. It was a warrior, like an intricately-sculptured chess piece, whose detail was intriguing on such a scale – `the minute links of the mail, the chiselled cat that crouched on the helm, the sword like a woman's pin. And all of it matt-white as chalk.

"I am here," the warrior cried in bell-like miniature tones. "What do you want of me?"

"Tell me how you came to be imprisoned in the crystal."

"My city was at war with another. The enemy took me in battle, and strove to gain, by torture, knowledge of a way our defences might be breached. When I would say nothing, a magician entered. He worked spells behind a screen. Then I was slain and my ghost sucked into the vase. Next moment, the magician summoned me forth, and they asked me again, and I told them everything."

"So," Subyrus remarked, "what you would not betray as a man, you revealed carelessly once you were a spirit."

"Exactly. Which was as the magician had foretold."

"Why? Because you were embittered at your psychic capture?"

"Not at all. But once within, human things ceased to matter to me. Old loyalties of the world, its creeds, yearnings and antipathies – these foibles are as dreams to those of us who dwell in the vase."

"Dwell? Is there room then, inside that little sphere, to dwell?"

"It would amaze you," said the warrior.

"No. But you may describe it."

"That is not normally one of the questions mortals ask when they summon us. They demand directions to our sepulchres, and ways to break in and come on our hoarded gold, or what hereditary defects afflict our line, in order that they may harm our descendants. Or they command us to carry out deeds of malevolence, to creep in small hidden areas and steal for them, or to frighten the nervous by our appearance."

"You have not replied to my question."

"Nor can I. The interior of this tiny vase houses seven thousand souls. To explain its microcosmic structure in mortal terms, even to one of the mighty Magician-Lords, would be as impossible as to describe colour to the stone-blind or music to the stone-deaf."

"But you are content," said Subyrus.

The warrior laughed flamboyantly.

"I am."

"You may return," said Subyrus, and uttered the dismissing incantation.

Subyrus progressed to a twentieth name, a twenty-first, a twenty-second. The twenty-third answered. This time a white philosopher stood in the air, his head meekly bowed, his sequin eyes whitely gleaming with the arrogance of great learning.

"Tell me how you came to be imprisoned in the crystal."

"A Tyrant acquired this vase and its spell. He feared me and the teachings I imparted to his people. I was burned alive, the spell activated, and my ghost entered the vase. Thereafter, the Tyrant would call me forth and try to force me to enact degrading tricks to titillate him. But though we who inhabit the vase must respond to a summons, we need not obey otherwise. The Tyrant waxed disappointed. He attempted to smash the vase. At length he went mad. The next man who called me forth wished only to hear my philosophies. But I related gibberish, which troubled him."

"Describe the interior of the vase."

"I refuse."

"You understand, my arts are of the kind which can retain you here as long as I desire?"

"I understand. I pine, but still refuse."

"Go then." And Subyrus uttered again the dismissing incantation.

It was past three o'clock. Altogether, six white apparitions had evolved from the blue vase. Subyrus had reached the fortieth name selected from the 'Tabulas Mortem'. He was almost too weary to speak it.

The atmosphere was feverish and heavy with rituals observed and magics pronounced. Subyrus's thin and beautiful hands shook slightly with fatigue, and his beautiful face had grown more skull-like. To these trivialities he was almost immune. Though exhaustion heightened his world-sated gravity.

He said the fortieth name, and the figure of a marvellous woman rose from the vase.

"Your death?" he asked her. She had been an empress in her day.

"My lover was slain. I had no wish to live. But the man who brought me poison brought also this vase under his cloak. When my soul was snared, he carried the vase to distant lands. He would call me up in the houses of Lords and bid me dance for his patrons. I did this, for it amused me. He received much gold. Then, one night, in a prince's palace, I lost interest in the jest. The prince appropriated the vase. When I begged leave to rest, the prince recited the incantation of dismissal, which the whipped man had revealed. Ironically, the prince was not comparably adept at the phrases of summoning, and could never draw me forth again."

The woman smiled, and touched at the white hair which streamed about her white robe.

"Surely you miss the gorgeous mode of your earthly state?" Subyrus said.

"Not at all."

"Your prison suits you, then?"

"Wonderfully well."

"Describe it."

"Others have told me you asked a description of them."

"None obliged me. Will you?"

But the woman only smiled.

Broodingly, Subyrus effected her dismissal.

He pushed the further names aside, and taking up the stopper of rose-opal, replaced it in the vase. The fermentation stilled within.

Slowly, the fire reproduced the darkness and scents that recalled Lunaria for the magician.

The vase was proven – and ready. The promise of such a thing would flatter even Lunaria. She had had toys before. But this – perverse, oblique, its potential elusive but limitless – it resembled Lunaria herself.

As the brazen bell-clocks of Vaim struck the fourth hour of black morning, an iron bird with chalcedony eyes (fifth of the Mechanicae) flew to the balconied windows of Lunaria's house.

The house stood at the crest of a hanging garden, on the eastern bank of the river.

Here Lunaria, honouring her name, made bright the dark, turning night into day with lamplight, singing, drums, harps and rattles. Her golden windows could be seen from miles off. "There is Lunaria's house," insomniacs or late-abroad thieves would say, chuckling, envious and disturbed. An odour of flowers and roast meats and uncorked wines floated over the spot, and sometimes firecrackers exploded, saffron, cinnabar and snow, above the roof and walls. But after sunrise the windows turned grey and the walls held silence, as if the house had burnt itself out during the night.

The iron bird rapped a pane with its beak.

Lunaria, heavy-eyed, opened her window. She was not astonished or dismayed. She had seen the bird before.

"My master asks when he may visit you."

Lunaria frowned.

"He knows my fee: a gift."

"He will pay."

"Let it be something unheard of, and unsafe."

"It is."

"Tomorrow then. At sunset."

4. Lunaria of Vaim

The sinking sun bobbed like a blazing boat on the river. Water and horizon had become a luminous scarlet, stippled with copper and tangerine. A fraction higher than the tallest towers of Vaim, this holocaust gave way to a dense mulberry afterglow, next to a denser blue, and finally, in the east, a strange hollow black, littered with stars.

Such a combination of colours and gems in the apparel of man or woman, or in any room of a house, would have been dubious. But in the infallible and faultless sky, were lovely beyond belief and almost beyond bearing.

Nevertheless, the sunset's beauty was lost on Subyrus, or rather, alleviated, dulled. At a finger's snap almost, he could command the illusion of such a sunset, or, impossibly, a more glorious one. It could not therefore impress or stimulate him, even though he rode directly through its red and mulberry radiance, on the back of a dragon of brass. The sixth of the Mechanicae, the dragon was equipped with seat and jewelled harness, and with two enormous wings that beat regularly up and down in a noise of metal hinges and slashed air. It caught the last light, and glittered like a fleck of the sun itself. In Vaim, presumably, citizens pointed, between admiration and terror.

A servant beat frantically on the door of Lunaria's bedchamber.

"Lady – *he* is here!"

"Who?" Lunaria inquired sleepily from within.

"The Lord Subyrus," cried the servant, plainly appalled at her forgetfulness.

On the terrace before the house, the dragon alighted. Subyrus stilled it with a single word of power. He stepped from the jewelled harness, and contemplated the length of the hanging garden. Trees precariously leaned over under their mass of unpicked fruit, the jets of fountains pierced shadowy basins that in turn overflowed into more shadowy depths beneath. Trellised night flowers were opening and giving up their scent. In Lunaria's garden no day flowers bloomed, and no man could walk. Sometimes the gardeners, crawling about the slanted cliff of the hanging garden to tend the growth and the water courses, fell to their deaths on the thoroughfare eighty feet- below. The only entrance to the house was through a secret door at the garden's foot, of whose location Lunaria informed her clients. Or from the sky.

The servant ran on to the terrace and cast himself on his knees.

"My lady is not yet ready – but she bids you enter."

The servant was sallow with fear.

Subyrus stepped through the terrace doors, and beheld a richly clad man in maddened flight down a stairway.

Lunaria had kept one of her customers late in order that Subyrus should see him. This was but a variation on a theme she had played before.

Near the stair foot, about to rush to a new flight – for these stairs passed right the way to the interior side of the secret door – the customer paused, and looked up in a spasm of anguish.

"You have nothing to dread from me, sir," Subyrus remarked. But the man went on with his escape, gabbling in distress.

"And I. Am I not to dread you?"

Subyrus moved about, and there Lunaria Vaimian stood, dressed in a vermillion gown that complemented one aspect of the sunset sky, her blonde hair powdered with crushed gilt.

She stared at Subyrus boldly. When he did not speak, she nodded contemptuously at the dining room.

"I am not proud," she announced. "I will take my fee at dinner. I am certain you will grant me that interim between my previous visitor and yourself."

The red faded on gold salvers and crystal goblets. Lunaria was wealthy, and she had earned every vaimii.

They did not converse, she and her guest. Behind a screen, musicians performed love songs with wild and savage rhythms. Servitors came and went with skilfully prepared dishes. Lunaria selected morsels from many plates, but ate frugally. Subyrus touched nothing. Indeed, no one alive could remember ever having seen him eat, or raise more than a token cup to his lips. Occasionally, Lunaria talked, as if to a third person. For example:

"How solemn the magician is tonight. Though more solemn or less than when he came here before, I cannot say."

Subyrus never took his eyes from her. He sat motionless, wonderful, awful, and quite frozen, like some exquisite graveyard moth, crucified by a pin.

"Are you dead?" Lunaria said to him at length. "Come, do not grieve. I will always be yours for a price."

At that he stirred. He placed a casket on the table between them, murmured something. The casket was gone. The vase of blue crystal glimmered softly in the glow of the young candles.

Lunaria tapped the screen with a silver wand, and the musicians left off their music. In the quiet, they might be heard scrambling thankfully away into the house.

Lunaria and the magician were alone together, with sorcery.

"Well," Lunaria said, "there was a tale in the city today. A blue vase in which thousands of souls are trapped. Souls which can inform of fabulous treasures and unholy deeds of the past. Courtesans who will reveal wicked erotica from antique courts. Devotees of decadent sciences. Geniuses who will create new books and new inventions. If they can be correctly persuaded. Providing one can call them by name."

"I could teach you the method," Subyrus said.

"Teach me."

"And so buy a night of your life?" Subyrus smiled. It was a melancholy though torpid smile. "I mean to have more than that."

"A week of nights for such a gift," Lunaria said swiftly. Her eyes were wide now. "You shall have them."

"Yes, I shall. And more than those."

He had got up from his chair, and now walked around the table. He halted behind Lunaria's chair, and when she would have risen, lightly he rested his long fingers against her throat. She did not try to move again.

The scents of ambergris and musk floated from her hair.

His obsession. The gnawing and only motive for his existence.

Obscuring from himself his true desire – the pang of her indifference, her challenge – he saw the road before him, the box in which he might lock her up. Physically, he had possessed her frequently. Such possession no longer mattered. Possession of mind, of emotion, of soul had become everything. The joy of actual possession, the intriguing misery of never being able to actually possess her again. And his fingers tightened about the contours of her neck.

She did not struggle.

"What will you do?" she whispered.

"Presently, remove the stopper of the vase. It is already primed to receive another ghost. Whoever expires now in its close vicinity will be drawn in. Into that microcosm where seven thousand souls dwell content. That enchanted world. They come forth haughtily, and retreat gladly. It must be curious and fine. Perhaps you will be happy there."

"I never knew you to lie, previously," Lunaria said. "You said the vase was a gift for me."

"It is. It will be your new home. Your eternal home, I imagine."

She relaxed in his grip and said no more. She remained some while like this, in a sort of limbo, before she was aware that his hands, rather than blotting out her consciousness, had unaccountably slackened.

Suddenly, to her bewilderment, Subyrus let her go.

He went away from her, about the table once more, and stopped, confronting the vase from a different vantage. An extraordinary expression had rearranged his face.

"Am I blind?" he said, so low she hardly made him out.

Youth, and of all things, panic, seemed swirling up from the darkened closets behind his eyes. And with those, an intoxication, such as Lunaria had witnessed in him the first night he had seen her, the first night she had refused him.

She rose and said sternly, "Will you not finish murdering me, my lord?"

He glanced at her. She was startled. He viewed her with a novel and courteous indifference. Lunaria shrank. What an ultimate threat had not accomplished, this indifference could.

"I was mistaken," he said. "I have been too long gazing at leaves, and missed the tree."

"No," she said. "Wait," as he walked towards the terrace doors, where the brazen dragon grew vague and greenish in a damson twilight.

"Wait? No. There is no more need of waiting."

The vase was in his hand. Sapphire flashed, and then went out as the dusk enclosed him.

The dragon heaved itself, with brass creakings, upright and abruptly aloft. Lunaria, rooted to the ground, watched Subyrus vanish into the sky above Vaim.

5. In Solitude

Somewhere in the hollow hill, a lion roared. It was a beast of jointed electrum, the seventh of the Mechanicae, activated and set loose by Subyrus on his return. Its task: to roam the chasm of the hill, a fierce guardian should any ever come there in the future, which was unlikely. It was unlikely because Subyrus, descending, had closed and sealed off the entrance to the hill by use of the eighth mechanism. The stone pavilion had folded and collapsed in unbroken and impenetrable slabs above the place. The periodic, inexhaustible roar of the lion from below was an added, really unnecessary deterrent.

And now Subyrus sat in his darkened hall, in his quartz chair. The fire did not burn. One lamp on a bronze tripod lit up the vase of blue crystal on a small table. The stopper lay beside it, and beside that a narrow phial with a fluid in it the colour of clear water.

Subyrus picked up the phial, uncorked, and leisurely drained it. It had the taste of wine and aloes. It was the most deadly of the six deadly poisons known on earth, but its nickname was Gentleness, for it slew without pain and in gradual, tactful, not unpleasant stages.

Subyrus rested in the chair, composed, and took the rose-opal stopper in his hand, and fixed his look on the vase.

He had exhausted the possibilities of the world long since. His intellect and body, both were sick with the sparse fare they must subsist on. There was no height he might not scale at a step, no ocean he might not dredge at a blink. No learning he had not devoured, no game he had not played. Thus, it had needed Lunaria to hold his horrified tedium in check, something so common and so ugly as a harlot's sneer to keep him vital and alive.

When the gate had opened, he had not seen it. He had nearly by-passed it altogether. He had sought a gift for Lunaria, then he had sought to trap her in the crystal, making her irrevocably his property and denying himself of her forever. Lunaria – he scarcely recalled her now.

Concentration on the minor issue had obscured the major. At the last instant, the truth had come to him, barely in time.

He had exhausted the world. Therefore he must find a second world of which he knew nothing. A world whose magic he had yet to learn, a world alien and unexplored, a world impossible to imagine – *the microcosm within the vase*.

Like a warm sleep, Gentleness stole over him. Primed to catch his ghost, the blue vase enigmatically waited. Perhaps nightmare crouched inside, perhaps a paradise. Even as the poison chilled it, Subyrus's blood raced with a heady excitement he had not felt for two decades and more.

In the shadows, a silver bell-clock struck a single dim note. It was the ninth of the Mechanicae, striking to mark the hour of the Magician-Lord's death.

And Subyrus sensed the moment of death come on him, as surely as he might gauge the supreme moment of love. He leaned forward to poise the rose-opal stopper above the lip of the vase. As the breath of life coursed from him, and the soul with it, unseen, was dashed into the trap of the crystal, the stopper dropped from his fingers to shut the gate behind him.

Subyrus, to whom existence had become mechanical, the tenth of his own Mechanicae, sat dead in his chair. And in the vase –

What?

Lunaria Vaimian had climbed the hill alone.

Below, at the hill's foot, uneasily, three or four attendants huddled about a gilded palanquin, dishevelled by cool winds and sombre fancies.

Lunaria wore black, and her bright hair was veiled in black. She regarded the fallen stone of the pavilion. Her eyes were angry.

"It is foolish of me," she said, "to chide you that you used me. Many have done so. Foolish also to desire to curse you, for you are proof against my ill-wishing as finally you were proof against my allure. But how I hate you, hate you as I love you, as I hated and I loved you from the beginning, knowing there was but one way by which I could retain your interest in me; foreknowing that I should lose you in the end, whatever my tricks, and so I have."

Leaves were blowing from the woods in the wind, like yellow papers.

Lunaria watched them settle over the stone.

"A thousand falsehoods," she said. "A thousand pretences. Men I compelled to visit me, (how afraid they were of the Magician-Lord), only that you might behold them. Gifts I demanded, poses I upheld. To mask my love. To keep your attention. And all, now, for nothing. I would have been your ghost-slave gladly. I would have let you slay me and bind me in the vase. I would have –"

The electrum lion roared somewhere beneath her feet in the hollow hill.

"There it is," Lunaria muttered sullenly, "the voice of my fury and my pain that will hurt me till I die; my despair, but more adequately expressed. I need say nothing while that other says it for me."

And she went away down the hill through the blowing leaves and the blowing of her veil, and never spoke again as long as she lived.

The Ghost
(in Two Letters)

The Ghost walked into the elaborate Dining Room of The Black Lion Hotel at exactly thirteen minutes past 7p.m. He was fashionably late.

He knew nobody there, he thought, apart from the 'Happy Couple'. Burn (was that an abbreviation of Bernard – or Burning? the Ghost had never known) was expansively greeting people by the free bar, under the coloured lights. Dinner itself was scheduled for eight o'clock. But where was she – for an anxious moment the Ghost could not quite recapture her name. But of course, it did come back. He was, after all, haunted by it, her name, the Ghost. Jolinda Franken, as it had appeared in the theatre programme; Joli for short. He didn't like 'Joli', he thought now. And did he like *her*? No, he thought. He only loved her. And there she was. In a silky orange outfit, presumably her 'Wedding Dress'. Dark hair streaming to her waist, honey-colour eyes wide with excitement and mascara. Cool and hot.

She had not seen him. But presumably she, not Burn, had sent the invitation.

The Ghost took one of the glasses of quite decent champagne from the edge of the bar. He was glad, even in the state he was in, he could grip the glass. Yet, when he sipped and swallowed a couple of times, the drink seemed flat and pale to him, a worn-out taste... He set the glass aside half consumed.

All the while, his eyes having located her, followed her – Jolinda, *Joli*. Was she beautiful? Was she what he had taken her for? Did he love her, even now?

Puzzled, he frowned, and someone in the adjacent crush of guests noticed him. "Hi! Cheer up! It's a *wedding*! I'm Steve –

and you?"

"Matthew," he said, thoughtless. Yes. He was Matthew.

But "Hi, Matt!" abbreviated the idiot, swigging back his full and foamy glass and reaching for a refill. "Who is it you know? Burny, or Joli?"

"Oh," he said vaguely, "both." Lies. He *knew* neither of them.

"He's a lucky fuck, isn't he, old Burn?"

"Yes," said the Ghost, reflectively.

"I mean, she's a looker – *and* an actor – I admit, never seen her in anything myself. But I don't do theatre much. Have you?"

"Yes," said the Ghost.

He did not add he had acted opposite Joli only last year, in that strange production in Edinburgh, *The Talking Street*. A silly play, badly written – except, almost annoyingly, for its radiant middle section. He had saved himself each night, he felt, making do through all the first half hour, just being - what was it? *Professional* – until you hit the buffers and exploded, three quarters of an hour before the interval. And that explosion had been his big scene with her. With Joli – Jolinda. Actors often got tangled up 'romantically' because passion had to burst out between them in a blaze, on stage, or in front of the camera. And presumably that was what had happened with them. From the tussle and fireworks on stage they were eventually decanted into the real sex scenes in his bed, there in the canny grey windings of that Scottish town. *She* knew it was nothing, really. The 'perfume and suppliance of a minute'. But for him it had meant rather more. Lovers, Matthew and Jolinda, Matt and Joli. (The twat with the abbreviation-fix had wandered off by now; the Ghost was alone again in the heart of the crowd.) Interesting, so much raucous festive life, and at its core, his deadness.

Was that then what finally he felt about her, his lover?

Only deadness? She did not seem, certainly, as he recalled – vulnerable, inflammatory, tender – *other*. No, this sexy young woman in her orange silk – and silk it was, for Burn, with his IT business, could afford it – she looked to the Ghost... only like – a memory.

Does it always come to this? Did I have to come to this to see the bitter truth of it, a tissue of lies, and like all tissues easily sodden with tears, or blood?

And now they were all to sit down to dinner. He moved, will-less, to the long tables, among the rest. Maybe there was a place marked for him? No, they hadn't gone that far. You simply sat where there was room. He took a chair way down from the cross-wise main table where Burn and she had sat. He could see her better from here. That was, she was farther off and so, oddly, clearly to be focussed on. Outside the tall windows the sun had started its long English set. The hotel garden, with its flowers and nicely-shaped tame trees, filled with shadow. The sky was pinkly gold, toning well with the orange dress; probably ordered, the sky, beforehand. And candles were being lit in here by the hotel staff.

There was perhaps a danger he would come to see, in the cameo of the candlelight, and after the sun's long fade, *only* her. Well, why not? She was why he had come here.

"Oh, hello," said a plump young woman to his left. "I'm Susie."

"Matthew," he said.

"Sorry, *what*? *Andrew* did you say?"

"Hey," (male voice), "Andrew, could you pass that wine carafe along, mate?"

He wondered if actually he *could*, but taking hold of the glassy jug, although his chilled fingers seemed to sink into its side as if into a cold jelly, he did make it move. That *was* love, then. Love could move a wine carafe, even now, just as Dante told you it moved the sun and the other stars.

His thoughts grew disorganised again. He wondered if he would be able to see that celestial movement, see the sun, for example, sinking inch by inch... But really, no doubt, he couldn't. All he would see was that dark-haired girl, beautiful in the most ordinary way, and shining with an almost painterly candle-ine lustre, as she clasped the hand of her husband. Burn.

Obviously, Matthew didn't know Burn. Only *of* him. But that was enough. Matthew stared. Burn was ugly, wasn't he? Was he? He was a creep with too-short hair and a fat mouth. In a couple more years *he'd* be fat. Or he'd work out in the gym and get muscle-bound. Or somebody would kill him for being the dubious business type Matthew had assumed Burn was.

The Ghost recollected when Jolinda first mentioned Burn. The recreated moments fell like thin cold slates into the Ghost's mind. It was when he and she came back from Edinburgh. The small part that had been mooted for him at the National had fallen through, as they so often did. His agent was talking about securing him work on a commercial – "Okay, Matthew, I know it *isn't* sixteenth sword-porter in *Lear*, but you'll get good money –"

"Off which you'll take your fifteen percent," Matthew added, so they had parted lukewarm to frigid. And then, going back to his room, Jolinda had gone out. And later she called him, "Sorry, Matthew. Someone I *have* to see. I'll be back – oh, midnight. Don't wait up, love." As if he were her bloody mother. She didn't come back anyway. (People always called each other, just 'met' – so direct. More honest – or more crass?) And next day they did meet, in the wine bar off the Strand. "Look, Matthew, I haven't been quite straight with you. I'm really sorry. It's just –"

It turned out she had been seeing Burn, (Bernard? Burning?), for some months before the Edinburgh stint. "I didn't know I'd meet someone like you... Oh, love," she added, sorrowful, acting her guts out, he was sure. "I've been a bitch. I couldn't resist. You're so tempting. And we've had a great time, haven't we? I couldn't have got through that crappy run if I hadn't been with you –"

"But now you're with him."

"Well, you see..." She paused, and drank down all the wine in her big glass – as if she desperately needed it, or more likely she wanted to finish it before she made a bolt for a taxi, Hampstead and Burn. "You see... he and I – we sort of – we may get married. I mean, not yet. In the summer. And so I can't go on seeing you, can I? I mean, it wouldn't be fair to him."

"Were you fair to him in Edinburgh?" he had asked her, deadly.

"No. Nor to you. Nor me. But – these things happen."

These things.

Before she could make her bolt for freedom he himself got up and left.

Yes, people always called, or texted each other, or emailed if you could afford a computer. Or they just met. He did try once, twice, to write to her, a letter. But he tore both of them up. Wasted paper.

She though had called him twice, since then. Once she was high – booze, or something, she liked her spliff. She seemed to be saying during these calls she would really enjoy one last sex session with him. Conceivably, he later thought, even after she got roped and tied with Burn, she might still like the occasional off-leash frolic with Matthew. But he wouldn't do that. They said women were the ones that got hurt, couldn't let go, made themselves miserable, died inside. Christ, what fucking rubbish. He had died, inside, the Ghost. You couldn't help where you loved, even if it was some illusion, some flake of candle-gleam, some echo of a once-off kiss or cry, a body smooth and soft as fur, a laugh you would know in blind darkness, the lamp of a golden eye that, for all those single seconds, saw only you.

He would always have to love her. He could let go – but *love* wouldn't let go of him. Love, which could move a wine carafe and the sun, had him firmly by its poisoned fangs and was shaking him to and fro. He would always love that stupid, brainless, ordinary scrap of flesh – a rag, a bone, and a hank of brunette hair –

"Are you done, sir?"

He glanced. A waitress leaning to him. There had been –

still was – something uneaten on his plate – paté, he guessed, a whisker of purple and green salad.

Am I done? "Yes," he said, "quite done."

And away it went, and here was something else. He stared at it, as he had stared at *her*, and could not translate what it was – meat? Pasta? – as he could not, any more, make out what *she* was.

The sun had gone down. A dark blue vitreous box covered the garden, with the twinkle of city lights beyond, the ever-reassuring pretence of mundane reality.

The Ghost reached for his glass. Found now he had neither the will nor the strength to raise it. But he would have to, he thought, because look, Burn and Joli were kissing in a sloppy adolescent way no actor, surely, would ever disgrace themself with in public. And then there was going to be a speech – the Best Man – who the hell was that? – oh, that grinning twot with a beard – and the Ghost too would be expected to clap and perhaps whistle, and lift and gulp champagne, and where had the second or third course gone?

The plump woman to his left was reaching right across him to take a chocolate from the thin woman on his right...

How bright the candles. But she, Joli, had not taught them their torchlike brightness. Her hair was dull and spoiled with the expensive treacle of hair products. Her eyes were dull as lead.

The audience laughed at the Best Man's best joke. God knew what it had been.

The Ghost remembered finding the invitation to this reception. It was in the hall of the flats. He saw it just after his agent called, on the crackling mobile that was running out of money, to say the commercial for the Energade Health Boost Drink had gone to another.

(A disco had started by now and figures flooded the dining room floor. He was partly conscious of their gesticulations, and the softly pulsating lights. And a clock sounded, or only a loud novelty watch – midnight, was it?)

'Love to welcome you,' the invite had said. 'This happy celebration' 'Our valued Guest'–

Why had she sent it to him? Or had it been Burn? Either of them – *why*? To torture? To gloat, to hurt and harm worse? To dance on his grave to the tune of the Wedding March, or the Death March: *Here comes the Died* –

"Is anyone sitting here?" somebody asked, under the laborious syntho base and drums.

"No," said the Ghost. As ever, he recognised his cue. He knew exactly when to leave. Invaluable, that, in an actor, perfect timing.

"That's the bloody weird part," said one uniformed man to another. "Several people apparently saw Haine. At least, early on, even three or four hours later. One girl said he had a really cool white shirt – and she described this shirt – and it was the one he was wearing. I saw it on him myself."

"Yeah," said the other uniform, "And that guy – Stephen something – he said he really liked Haine's wrist-band, asked him where he got it, but never had a reply."

Their drank their coffee. (The canteen never did it quite right, too frothy, not strong enough. Thank God in a few more hours there was a chance at *Starbucks*.)

"Well, what I think," said the first uniform, "he went to the reception, and then nipped home and finished up."

"Yeah but – well, they're hushing all this up, aren't they? The SOCO, he was in a right state. Never saw him like that – and the T.O.D. –"

"It can't be anything else, can it?" Flat as one more cold slate, these words. "And a wedding – all of them drinking. People see what they expect to. Even she –"

"Yeah. Ms Franken."

"She's Mrs Burnley now."

"Yeah, well, whatever. *She* said she saw Haine. Said she was amazed he was there. She agreed she sent him an invite, but she meant him to take that as a warning, to let him know she *had* got hitched, and no hard feelings. Never reckoned he'd show."

"Fucking slag," said the first uniform.

"Took the words right out of my mouth," agreed his companion. "Shall we hit the road?"

They had been called to the premises, (Haine's flat), around midnight of the same evening that Joli Franken and Burnley held their Wedding Party at The Black Lion. And the party, in fact, had still been in full swing on the other side of London. It was a classic clue that alerted the people in the flat below Haine's (*flats* – each one room, with a scrawny kitchenette and a shared toilet down the passage). The clue was reminiscent of Hardy's *Tess of the D'Urbervilles* – that was, blood seeping through the ceiling above. The lot downstairs found it on returning from the pub, supposing it red paint at first. But as it kept on spreading they didn't want it in their take-away. Very wise.

The corpse was sitting upstairs, in a good suit and a really good white shirt. He hadn't fallen off his chair, just leaned a bit. He had swallowed half a bottle of a choice red wine, and about twenty-three generally-prescribed sleeping tablets. He had also cut open the vein of his left wrist with a razor blade, very very efficiently, slicing longways *not* across, which was a pretty infallible method. There were no preliminary hesitant scratches or cuts, either. Matthew Haine had known exactly what he meant to do, and had done it with the adroitness of an actor who had, reasonably often, acted suicide on the stage.

He was recently bathed, and his hair washed. He was deodorised, shaved, and with a touch of mid-range cologne. The clothes, as stated, were of good quality. And he had somehow managed, even when consciousness departed, to keep the blood off them. He really had been got up for a party. It was just he hadn't gone to it. Or had he? This was the nagging question, except, of course, you did not want to ask it. He had *died*. And time of death was now established as being, at the latest, seven o'clock that evening. And so, when he walked into The Black Lion Hotel dining room – he could *not* have done so. He was already that smart, clean corpse, which had drugged and bled the life out of itself, in the room whose door the police broke down at midnight.

The 'copper wrist-band' spotted at the party was uncomfortable too. Those who subsequently mentioned it soon tried to brush it off their awareness. Because it might, in some sordid supernatural tale, have been an accurate cipher for Haine's blood-starved, blood-encrusted wrist. A lot of the guests had thought him very pale. "Dishy," one girl said, "sort of goth-vampire." Here and there one or two of them had been noting Haine as late as 11.30 p.m. And then – he just hadn't seemed to be there. He was gone.

So. If you could credit the idea, even if never, never – *ever* would you *truly* credit the idea as a *fact* – Matthew Haine had killed himself, and then arrived as a stone-dead ghost at the wedding party. The Ultimate Spectre at the Feast.

He hadn't left a farewell message. There was just the invitation to the reception tucked in the breast pocket of his jacket – which, when they broke in the door, fell out and landed a few inches clear of the waterfall of spent blood. Very gracious it was, the invite. And almost just like all the other invites sent to all the other three hundred odd guests. His name was spelled out in curlicues, and led to such phrases as: *Love to welcome you* and *Happy celebration*, addressing the recipient, at the end, as *'Our valued Guest'*. Yes, that was really the stumbling block, the problem. Matthew Haine – and who else would have done such a thing? – had, before placing the card in his pocket, changed two letters in those last three words. Crossing out the 'u' and the 'e' in the word *Guest*, he had rewritten them as an 'h' and an 'o'. Which accordingly left the invitation to read, significantly or not, 'Our valued Ghost.'

The Ghost of the Clock

I don't believe in ghosts. Assuming there is a soul, why should it hang around here, if there is somewhere else it has to go? Oh, maybe there are recordings of past events that get left behind. Maybe even extreme emotions leave a kind of *colour*, like a stain. But that's it.

So, this isn't a ghost story. Although it has a ghost.

My name is Laura. And there came a time when clever Laura found herself in bad financial straits – unable to pay the rent on her so-called flat in London, (one room, and use of a bathroom down the hall), or for anything very much. My parents were long gone – my dad to that Somewhere Else I mentioned; my mother to southern France with her "New Bloke". She'd used him like camouflage and was virtually unfindable.

I ended up accepting the offer of a roof from my aunt.

Jennifer was my father's only sister. I'd seen her, once or twice, in childhood, but she had disliked my mother devotedly, so it hadn't been very often. I knew she had a house on the coast – I won't say where, but it was a good address. I'd been a bit surprised to get her letter.

It was a long journey, and the train stopped outside some picturesque country halt for about fifty minutes extra. My fellow passengers grumbled, but otherwise just carried on as usual, beetling over their ghastly twittering laptops, honking away into their bloody mobile phones. I went to the buffet and got a double gin and tonic. It was eleven thirty a.m., but what the hell.

In the afternoon, when I had arrived and was waiting for a taxi, what struck me was the light.

I've heard the light is different – better – in Greece. Having never been there, I don't know if that is true. But certainly the

English light that curtained the seaside town was sheer and crystal *clean*, as if the sea cast it up fresh-spun. When we drove out of the station and off up the bumping, winding, narrow roads to the hills, I looked at all the May-green woods and fields burning in this light, and the birds darting over like arrows with gold-tipped flights, and then the vast sweep of the sea itself, bluer than the sky.

This was a beautiful spot. The sort of non-resort the sensitive, England-orientated rich go to, for their holidays. Only I wasn't on holiday. And decidedly I was not rich.

Soon, we saw the house.

"Fair old place, that," said the driver, who until then had been unchatty.

I felt embarrassed. I didn't want to say my aunt lived here. I toyed with the idea of telling him I'd applied for the job of scullery maid, but that would be about a century out of date. Secretary, then, or personal assistant?

Lamely, I said, "Yes, isn't it."

And he and I left it at that.

We went up a winding drive, and the house, which had appeared so dramatically on a hill-top, now vanished behind broad stands of oak, pine and hornbeam, and clouds of rhododendrons, blazing white and crimson.

Really, I suppose, it wasn't so big – not grounds or an estate, more a huge garden.

We passed under flowery terraces and roses, and then there was the house again, across a blank green oval of lawn.

It was a flat-fronted building, brown-skinned, with a large porch mounted on a little raised terrace, with a statue. I added up twelve windows along the top storey before I stopped counting.

All right, it wasn't a stately home, but it was much more than just a *home*.

There was a garden all round, but to one side the land dropped in terraces, and over there, through the boughs of a cedar-tree, the turquoise ocean appeared again, less than half a mile away.

The driver helped me with my bags, then left me. I watched the cab rattle off, as I stood at the door. I'd expected by now a servant in costume to come out to look down his nose at me. But no one had come, and when I finally jangled the old-fashioned bell, nothing happened either. Then I saw the electric bell hiding under the other one, and tried that.

Well, I did anticipate an employed door-opener of some sort at least.

But what eventually came was my Aunt Jennifer.

She looked at me with all the contempt of any imagined butler, before the falsest of false smiles oozed up her wrinkled face.

"Laura! How lovely. Do come in."

This was my aunt's big secret. She was mean. Wealthy people sometimes are, surprisingly so. It's how they stay wealthy, possibly. (I don't know how she was well-off when we hadn't been. I think it was from some kind of exclusive legacy.)

Really, if I'd thought, I'd have remembered enough from my childhood. I wasn't a stupid kid, less stupid probably than I've become since growing up. Twenty-five years back, when I was nine or so... That weird thing over the individual ice-cream, for example. "Just eat half, Laura, and save some for later. It will keep in the ice-box..." But my aunt was mean not only in the monetary sense, but in her ways.

She had hated my mother. And I was, after all, half my mother, even if, as far as I was concerned, I'd really only ever had one parent, and he was dead.

I loved my father. He was kind and gentle, a dreamer, who liked music, and silence. Death beglamoured him for me even more – after the agony went off. He had had a heart-attack the night before I was twenty.

Conceivably, I would have liked to get on with Jennifer, who had been his sister and so was, as I was, also partly him.

My bags got left in the wide walnut-brown hallway. We

went into a sunny, rather dusty room, with long windows looking out over another lawn, the cedar and the sea. The windows weren't very clean. All that – the dust, the windows, startled me. I mean, I'd lived regularly in a tip, but I didn't expect that here – and definitely not amid this antique furniture and these Persian rugs.

The gardens too had been very well kept, trees neatly trimmed to proper *shapes*, and the lawns mowed to within an inch of their lives. So she *did* have a gardener.

My aunt told me I must sit down.

"You must sit down, Laura. You must be quite tired. But a cup of tea will put you right."

Then, another little shock. Jennifer crossed to an ornate eighteenth century sideboard and switched on an electric kettle roosting there. Next to this was set a covered tray. Presently, Jennifer brought everything to a coffee-table between the two white brocade sofas.

Unveiled, the tray held a plate of two dry chicken sandwiches, constructed perhaps in the early morning, two plain biscuits, and a banana past its first flush of youth. This feast was for me.

As she poured the boiled water on to the tea (bags of course) in the tarnished silver pot, I began to see the light. The garden she had kept up – for 'appearances'? But she had no help in the house, or very little. No one to dust or clean or shine up the silver, let alone open the door. No one came in to cook meals, either, or even make the poor old girl a cuppa.

She was sixty-seven by my reckoning. She looked older, having one of those faces that get easily creased.

"I've given you a west-facing room, Laura. It gets the last of the sun."

Fine, I thought. Chilly first thing and too hot on a summer's evening.

"Well, you must tell me all about yourself."

I glanced at her, and she sat there, like a slightly overweight Venus flytrap.

Shouldn't I think of her like that? Should I be sorry for her, all on her own, and not even able to afford, or too *afraid* to afford, despite her house, domestic help or even decent teabags? Had she fallen on hard times? Was she lonely? Did she truly want to know me? She must have known my whereabouts at least, because her letter had come straight to me. But before that, I hadn't seen or heard from her since the funeral.

"There's not much to say, Aunt Jennifer."

"But you've made a bit of a mess of your life, haven't you?"

Yes, Venus flytrap.

"Not really. Companies are folding all the time in London. Everywhere. It's the economic climate."

"I blame these computers," she said darkly. "This Internet thing."

"Works of the Devil," I heard myself mutter.

"Always wanting something for nothing," she concluded, as if I either hadn't said anything, or simply endorsed her own suspicions. "And this man - *Even*, was he called?"

"Eden."

I sensed she thought I'd had an affair with my boss.

"He let you down," she said.

"No, actually –"

"American," she appended scathingly. "Oh, they did plenty of that, letting girls down, I can tell you, in the last war."

I wondered what she'd got up to during the Blitz – to sound so pissed-off. She would have been a bit young, wouldn't she?

"Eden was great, and when the sh... when the trouble started, he did everything he could to put things right for all of us. It wasn't his fault. But if you mean did I sleep with him? No. He was very happily married."

"Oh yes," she said. She managed to look disgusted at my directness, and wisely aware I was lying, both at once. "However, you lost your flat and your job. And I gather you have no savings."

This was like an interview – perhaps by the police.

"I didn't have very much anyway. Living in London is very expensive."

"I'm sure it is. Well, never mind. You're here now. I'll take care of you."

I felt in that moment like a child – small, thirty-four-year-old orphan. I wanted to say, *Stuff it*. Get up and stalk out, perhaps throwing the half-dead banana at the dirty windows first. But I didn't. I had less than five hundred pounds in the bank and less than forty in my wallet. My three bags contained every scrap I owned that I hadn't sold for next to nothing. Because of my almost freelance status with the company, my tax situation was in a muddle. I wasn't highly skilled, had no tremendous talents, and for every job I was likely to seek, there would be at least fifteen other eager or desperate applicants. It used to be people over fifty who had difficulty getting work. Then it was forty. I'd begun to believe the age had recently fallen even lower. I'd been stacking shelves in the supermarket when Jennifer wrote to me.

If I wanted a breathing space, I would have to put up with her.

After all, it wasn't so bad, was it? The house was uncared for but lush, the gardens glorious, and the beach and swim-in-able sea just down the hill.

I said, I'm stupid now.

"Well, Laura, if you've finished your meal, perhaps you'd better take your bags up and settle into your room."

Dismissed.

"Okay. Thanks, I will." I rose and said, feeling I still had to, "It's very kind of you –"

The horrible creeping smile squeezed over her face again. She was all over-powdered and rosy like a girl gone quite wrong, and her hair was thick and old and coarse and too brown, so I knew it was from dye, and not a very good one either. Naturally.

Oh God, she made me sick. I was *allergic* to her.

She said, "That's all right, Laura. I know you had an

unfortunate time with your mother, that can't have helped you. Anyway, pop upstairs now." She gave me directions to the room, with no intention of stirring herself to show me. Then: "I usually eat about seven. You'll find all the things ready for you in the kitchen. It's easy to find, the back-stair is just along from your room, on the left."

I checked.

"You mean the way to the kitchen?"

"Yes," she said.

Hold on, I thought. Am I hearing what I think? She plans for me to go down and fix dinner. Scullery maid, did I say? But no, it isn't that. She just means there's some sort of cold stuff ready, and I'm to bring it upstairs to save her aged legs.

"I'm afraid," she added, arch and acid, "I don't have a microwave. You'll have to manage the cooking without. I've never accepted those things are safe."

I found my room without problems. It wasn't a maid's room – those, if there were any, were up in the attics, I expect. But it could have won a prize for Smallest Guest Bedroom in Britain.

After I'd propped my bags against the single bed, I edged past a huge, bear-like wardrobe, and stared out of the window.

The view was good – inland, to fields and beech woods honey-spread by a westering sun. It was already almost five.

I knew that from my watch, not from any clock. The house *had* clocks – I'd passed one in the narrow side corridor, which led to this very room. But none in my bedroom. She had presumably anticipated I'd bring my own.

There was a bathroom to the right of the room, down an awkward step. It had bath and lavatory and so on, even a hand-held shower-attachment. There was some soap, (not new), and a couple of towels, and toilet-paper, bright green and rather cheap. The bathroom also had a tear in the lino floor-covering and some loose wall tiles. But the flush worked, and the water ran hot. Why complain? I'd lived with worse.

But after I'd showered and re-dressed, I sat on my lumpy

bed, smouldering in my anger.

She wanted a skivvy. I knew it. Had I known before I came? No. There had been nothing in the letter to indicate any of this. Or... could I be wrong?

All right, then. Give it till tomorrow. And then, if necessary, take off. Because it would be better to do almost anything than become maid-of-all-work for my Aunt Jennifer. Oh – I could bloody murder her –

It was then that the clock clanged in the corridor.

So we come to the clock.

I'd barely looked at it on my way to the bedroom, but when I came out again to locate the kitchen stair, I first walked back the short distance down the corridor, and stared at the thing.

It was the ugliest clock, perhaps the most ugly piece of furniture I have ever seen.

It was about ten feet tall, made of some black old-looking wood that had a strong odour of must or rot to it, uncarved or decorated, except for a painting on its high-up face. A type of grandfather clock, I deduced, but the oddest thing was that, where in such a clock there's usually a glass panel to look through, and so observe the swinging pendulum – even a door that can be unlocked in order to adjust the mechanism – in this model there was not, only the closure of unrelieved wood. Nor did the clock make any working sound. None of that deep *tugk-tockk* you hear so much of in a good atmospheric period radio play. It had only made one noise, the single monstrous clang.

As I said, the face of the clock did have a decoration. First there were, in black, the Roman numerals. The hands were both firmly clamped to the VI, which was six all right – the actual time – but surely, if they had reached six and the clock had struck five minutes ago, the hands should now have moved on? I watched them awhile, and nothing happened. VI was all it was going to be.

To return to the decoration, though. The left side of the numerals was a woman's face done like a mask. The style was old-fashioned – it looked eighteenth century to me. It was also nasty in some way I couldn't quite determine – save that, since it *was* a mask, though it had smiling red lips, the eyes were gaps of black, and in the black of each gap was a tiny silver point, so little that, from that far below I couldn't see what it was – but they looked like *pins*.

On the other side of the clock-face was the image of something even less appealing. I took it for a monkey's head, this one wizened and evil-looking.

Having inspected the clock, I turned round and found the back stair, a twisting treacherous corkscrew lit by a couple of the narrowest windows. The kitchen was along a passage at the bottom.

Any doubts were cancelled. Everything was shoved on the big wooden table, ready for preparation, vegetables, potatoes, a (shop-made) fruit pie. Placed in the middle was a postcard with a view of the town, on the back of which were instructions about the stove, the cutlery and plates, and where the fridge-freezer was with the sausages.

Apparently my aunt had faith I could cook. But she also perhaps knew how ineptly, or why hadn't she wanted something more elaborate?

II

"This is all a little cold, Laura. Did you heat everything thoroughly?"

I said nothing, refusing now to play her game.

Before she started her critique of the food, (including its late arrival), she'd commented on the *size* of my meal – "*Two* sausages, Laura? And all those peas – Surely a young woman needs to watch her figure... and I thought I had left a cabbage out. The frozen peas were for Sunday."

Everything was fifth rate anyway. The sausages tasteless, the potatoes floury. Even the pie was flavoured mostly with chemicals and had about three apple slices in it.

We ate in the dining-room. This was another wide chamber,

with windows giving on the lawn with the view of the sea. As daylight sank away, pink clouds and swallows came on, and then a high, blue-green dusk. By then I'd been back down for the apple-less pie, and down again to make instant coffee.

She didn't ask me to do this, she told me. And I obeyed.

And I kept thinking, I can't arrange a thing tonight. I'll sort all this out in the morning.

Am I spineless? Less that than rather tired.

The instant coffee, too, was not the kind that makes people alert, sexy and wise in the adverts. It was the kind you use to scare out the drains.

After dinner she opened the French doors, however, and said we should have an after-dinner stroll on the lawn.

Was she showing me what I would be missing if I rebelled and ran away?

The sea lay far out, adrift in the sky, dark now, and darker than the luminous dusk, just as it had been more blue than the sky, before. The air was fresh and pure and smelled of roses, clematis, and salt.

"Tomorrow," said Aunt Jennifer, "perhaps you should make an early start. I'm afraid everything has got very dirty. Perhaps you should begin downstairs. You won't forget to clean the windows, will you?"

I drew a breath of the beautiful air.

"Where in your letter to me," I said, "exactly, did you specify that if I came to stay in your house, I would automatically become your cook and cleaner?"

"Housekeeper, Laura."

"I see. Did you mention a fee, then, the wages I'd get for being your – er – housekeeper? I seem to have missed all that. "

"Oh, I can't afford to pay you. I can't afford that sort of luxury. But you're getting your keep, aren't you?"

I was, despite everything, dumbfounded by her relaxed demeanour. I thought, wildly, she's been dreaming this up, perhaps, for years. Why? To get at my *mother*? At me? What had *I* ever done to her?

We'd been walking along the lawn all this time. As if engrossed in the most ordinary, friendly dialogue.

Now, around the bushes, the drop opened before us, a sailing away of the hill in air and darkness, quite dramatic. And I thought, Shall I just push the old cow over? But naturally I would never do that.

And then she said, "Did you see the clock in the corridor near your door?"

"What has –?"

"Didn't you think it rather peculiar?"

I said nothing, less from stern resolve than an inability to keep up with this.

"It has a story. That clock."

She was, my aunt, a very dumpy, unattractive figure in her sensible jumper, skirt and shoes. Yet in the last of the twilight, she was melting to a shadow of her former self, a dumpy *solid* shadow, lit now and then by a smeary flash of eyes.

"This house was built about 1900, only about a hundred years ago. Some playwright owned it. Some homosexual creature. He used to collect eccentric bits of furniture. I'm sure I have no interest in him, or in them, and none of them remain. Apart from the clock. The clock was one of his finds, and it's always been in the house. Quite a curiosity. One can't move it, you see."

Despite myself, I reacted. "Why not?"

"Because it was nailed to the floor of the upper storey, and in such a way, it would mean all the floor-boards and the joists would have to come up, to pry it loose. I was warned about this. It's an eyesore, of course," she announced. "I don't imagine even you, Laura, with your extreme notions, would like it. At one time the previous tenants had it boarded up – but all that gave way, and well, I couldn't afford to have it done again."

"And besides, I added, "it's only in the corridor that leads to the back stairs."

"Yes, quite."

Dark now. Night had come. The swallows were finished and instead the odd bat was flitting over. I could just hear the sea, its slow sighing, so intimate, so eternally indifferent.

Jennifer said, "Did you see the two images painted on the face?"

"Yes."

"Youth and Age, they're called."

An explanation disconcertingly formed in my mind. The *mask* was youth – rather a quaint idea, I supposed – a hollow false face that didn't last and eventually had to come off to reveal what was truly there inside. Which was the evil-looking *monkey*? Yes, old age, the mischievous joker. It could make you ugly. *Animal.*

Was that precisely what was happening to Jennifer – mask ripped away, the mad beast beginning to show...?

But she said, "All a lot of nonsense, of course. The interesting part is about the main body of the clock, the area inside the wooden frame."

The day had been warm. It was getting chilly now. A stiff light wind, blowing in over cooling seas, iced down my arms and through my T-shirt, and between my sandalled toes crept the breaking dew.

"So?" I said. Why was I indulging her in this? What the hell was the matter with me? Tell her to fly off the hill, the old witch. Or I should. God, there must be a pub around here somewhere – light, warmth, sanity and booze –

Jennifer said, "It's haunted. The clock."

She said it with enormous relish. As if she was counting it, like her money.

"Oh I see."

"It's only a story, evidently," she glibly said, facile in her absolute certainty she was getting to me. Was she? I didn't believe in – "I found the history in an old book once, a library book, or I could show you – An unpleasant little tale. Most unpleasant."

"How do you know the clock in the book is the same

clock?"

"Oh, the estate agent told me years ago, when I was buying the place. In case I found out, I imagine, and got ratty. Then when I read the story in the book, I recognised it was my clock, or rather the *house* clock. And the book gave a lot more details."

"You're obviously dying to tell me."

I tried to sound patronising, but really just wished I'd keep quiet.

She would tell me anyway.

But then Jennifer said, "Well, I don't know, Laura. At this late hour. I remember what a nervous child you were – I don't want to alarm you. It's not a nice story. It might keep you awake. And you'll need your sleep if you're to get an early start on the house in the morning."

And then – *then* – the foul old bag turned on her clumpy heel and marched away from me up the lawn, towards her economically faint-lit house. Leaving me with only the cold night and the indifferent sea, and the uneasy suspicion that if I didn't hurry after her, she might lock me out all night.

Had I been nervous as a child? Not especially. And yet there was a kind of something in me, always had been, a sort of feral awareness of – God knew what. Maybe that's why, in part, I don't believe in the supernatural. It's less that I don't than that I *won't*.

My father had been sensitive. Not afraid or cowardly, I don't mean that. But the rubbish of the world could get to him, truly upset him; reported cruelties in other countries, or my wretched mother... It was why he'd died, I think. Worry, and trying not to worry, or rather never passing the worry on to her, because he couldn't, to me because he wouldn't.

I *hated* thinking of him like this, now, sitting up in the awful bed, wondering – I couldn't help it – if Jennifer, who had been his elder by three years, had tried to frighten him when he was a little boy. They'd both been kids when the war started, and evacuated together to some farm. I had this picture of them in the unknown dark, he only about four or five, and *she* telling him horror stories.

All the time I sat there, I too was in the dark. There was no side-lamp, just the overhead bulb with the switch by the door. Another form of economy? Since, unless you wanted to sleep with the light full in your eyes, you had to turn it off before getting into bed.

Then the clock went off again. And I nearly jumped out of the house, let alone my skin.

This time, it clanged twice. But it was only just past midnight, according to my luminous alarm-clock.

I thought, (irrationally?) that's the other reason she's put me in here. So her damn clock can keep me awake.

Then, I heard the rustling sound.

Okay, I admit my hair stood on end. There I was in the spooky dark, alone, and here was this crepuscular little noise suddenly coming to join me, over there, by the door.

It's mice I decided.

So I switched on the torch I'd had the sense to bring, conjuring country lanes by night, and shone it full at the doorway, expecting to pick up two or more little bright mouse eyes.

It wasn't mice.

There, pushed in under the door, were some sheets of paper.

I gaped at them. Then I got out of bed, crossed the intervening three feet of room, and picked the papers up. Then I switched on the overhead light.

The papers were handwritten, and I knew the writing, over-ornamented and tightly cramped, as if nothing must slip between the words or letters. It was hers. I'd seen it on her letter.

Disbelieving, despite the rest, (and the obvious fact she must have crept soundless to my door in order to slot this under it), I read:

Laura, I remembered I had copied this from the library book I told you about. I thought you might be intrigued. I've pushed it under your door in order not to disturb you. Read it in the morning. No doubt, to your sophisticated mind, it will seem a very silly tale.

How was that for contradictory malice? Also, she *knew* I'd be 'disturbed', unless I was stone *deaf* and hadn't heard the clangs of the clock.

I sat down on one of the bed's rocky humps, and read the remainder of the hand-written pages, which detailed carefully the story of the clock. They did read as if these passages had come from a book.

The clock, the text informed me, dated back to 1768, and had been made in France. In those days it had had the normal glass window, through which the pendulum might be seen, and the whole front of the lower clock might be opened in order to reach the workings. The face, then and now, was decorated with a macabre motif then current in decadent Paris, and entitled *Youth and Age,* represented in either respective case by a mask and a distorted, monkey-like human head.

During the French Revolution, the clock reached England, brought over, for some inane reason, by fleeing aristocrats. And in 1820, it passed into the possession of an English family named Trente. They placed it in their country house, somewhere in the vicinity of Lathamfold.

Due to various reverses, there came in time to be only two females left to represent the Trente family, a young woman, Sabia Trente, and her elderly aunt, Eugenia. Both had experienced rather irksome lives, the old aunt unmarried and impoverished, dependant on her young niece, who, apparently no longer rich, and quite plain, was herself without hope of catching a suitable man.

The book, or Jennifer, omitted to say much about the existence they led together in their failing country mansion, rubbing each other up the wrong way all the while, since they didn't like each other at all, due to some quarrel in the family. Somewhat in the manner of an antique Cinderella, the aged aunt, (she was sixty-odd, which must have been more like eighty in those days), was soon consigned to the servants quarters, and required to carry out quite menial work uncomplimentary to her years and status. Sabia Trente, meanwhile, lost no opportunity to *'heap contumily'* on the old girl's head, and in the end they were deadly enemies.

By the year Sabia was thirty, youth's bloom gone and her last illusory chance of marriage with it, they occupied the mansion with only one actual servant. The grounds had run to seed and weed. Local farmers grazed their pigs and sheep on the meadows, and paid the Trentes a pittance to do it. The house was in bad repair, some of its roof down, and all its treasures sold.

All, that is, but for the French clock.

It would seem there was some sentimental or superstitious reason why Sabia Trente had *not* sold the clock, which might have brought a fair price as a curiosity, having become, of its kind, quite rare.

However, rather than be sold, something else happened with the clock.

One night, aunt and niece had a real falling out. For years they'd been arguing, but on this particular night it came to blows. Sabia struck first, slapping the old woman across the face and head so hard she fell down. It was then that Auntie Eugenia reached for a fire-iron. She in turn struck her niece a blow *'harsh enough it clove the brain-case in twain'*.

Skull fracture accomplished, Auntie, in the rational panic of the amateur turned professional, dragged her niece to the tall clock, standing handy, undid the door, and with the super-strength of fear and rage, stuffed Sabia inside. *Then*, Eugenia hauled the younger woman upright, propped her, (presumably smashed head lolling and bleeding) against the pendulum – which naturally at once stopped moving – slammed shut the door and locked it. She then flung the key in the fire, where the heat soon deformed and disguised it. Last of all, the inventive homicide pulled down one of the frowsty curtains and slung it right over the clock, draping it from top to toe, and thus hiding its new grisly contents from view.

Jennifer's library book calmly commented that the old servant woman, if she at all noticed the clock had been shrouded, paid no attention, being used to the 'eccentricities of her mistresses'. And when the dead body began to stink? The clock apparently held most of that safely inside. The occasional whiff was put down to dead rats in the wall, an occurrence of charming frequency.

Not even the disappearance of one of the Trentes was much noted. Both Sabia and Eugenia had long since ceased to frequent the village, or even the church. If the visiting pigs or farmers failed to see Sabia, trailing through the long grass of her estate in her ruined yellow gown, they doubtless only thought she had given up trailing, too, with her other renunciations.

As for the servant, *'she asked no questions'*.

Incredibly, if all this were a fact, Eugenia then lived on in the Trente house for five more years before she *'died of an apopplexy'*. The servant promptly left, stealing a few squalid items to assist her passage. Others came after the funeral, to clear and tidy the house. And that was when, of course, they found what was in the clock, a partly-mummified, partly-skeletal cadaver, held rigidly upright in its black-stained, pale yellow rags – which, once the curtain was fully off, was displayed as clearly as a mannequin in a shop window.

Some sort of investigation took place. It revealed, perhaps not amazingly, an account of what had actually happened, penned, (boastfully?), by Aunt Eugenia in her journal, and hidden in a concealed bureau drawer.

The clock meanwhile was broken open and the corpse removed and buried. A type of exorcism was reportedly performed. Exactly why was not specified. After that, the clock was sold at last, and went to unknown buyers.

Thereafter nothing was heard of it, until early in 1909, when it reappeared at an auction, boarded all round with plain wood, and said very definitely to be haunted. This was when the gay playwright, who had formerly inhabited Jennifer's house, saw the clock and collected it.

His name was Shelley Terrence, and he had enjoyed some stage successes during the Art Nouveau era, enough to set him up financially and leave him bored. At first he was *'fascinated'* by the clock, inviting his friends of all sexes down for weekends to see it. But then they, and he, changed their minds.

'Terrence alleged,' said Jennifer's book, *'that several of his guests had been woken at night in terror, on more than one occasion, by ghastly moans and cries issuing from the sealed-up stem of the clock. One of the guests, a certain Lady Devere Payne, claimed to have witnessed a pallid figure, in a yellow gown of the early Victorian years, lurching through the bedroom, from wall to wall – through both of which walls she passed unhindered – and wearing besides a scarlet, fringed turban that, the lady subsequently realised, was really a mass of wetly-matted hair and blood.'*

The guests fled, but worse was to follow.

Coming in late one evening, Terrence was standing talking with his manservant in the downstairs hall, when both men heard a *'creaking and groaning as of a ship at sea in high wind.'* Looking up, each man saw the same thing – the clock, which seemed to be moving quite rapidly across the top of the main staircase. It disappeared before reaching the stairs' opposite side, but not before they had also noticed shreds of yellowish material *'billowing'* from the spot where its door might have opened, had it still had one.

When they had gathered enough courage, Shelley and his man went to the room where the clock had originally been set down, and found it in a much altered position.

No surprise, another exorcism followed. After which, it seemed, Terrence was advised against ousting the clock, and instead recommended to have it ported to a back corridor, and there nailed down with long iron farriers' nails, right through the floor-boards and a joist.

This did seem to end the clock's personal activity. But by then a name had been given the ghost – the Woman in Yellow. And she herself did not leave Shelley Terrence entirely alone.

She would manifest at random awful moments, such as when he stood shaving, and saw her abruptly behind him in his mirror – a sight that so jolted him, he said, that he nearly cut off his ear. At last his nerves broke down, and he quit the house for America.

Thereafter another family, the pragmatic Jordans, lived there for a number of decades. It was they who had boarded up the clock entirely, but also they swore they did not credit ghosts, and experienced nothing unusual during their tenure.

And after the Jordans, though the book didn't mention her, came my aunt.

Perched on the hillock in the bed, I put the pages down, all this information meticulously copied, (or *invented*? – it didn't seem likely), by my own aunt.

That she was trying to frighten me, however, was pretty obvious. It was evidently all of a piece with her design for me here. To humiliate me and make me her unpaid servant – a curious reversal of Sabia and Eugenia Trente – wasn't sufficient. No, she wanted to give me nightmares, too.

Why did she have it in for me? I thought back, cautious. All I could recall was a dim, much younger version of Jennifer, making snide remarks about my mother's behaviour, Jennifer's nagging voice gnawing away at my father, and more sharply at child-me – "Don't do that, Laura. That grass will get your skirt dirty, and heaven knows, your mother won't have anything ready for you to change into." Oh, and Dad's funeral. When she stood there, dabbing her bright, dry, hard eyes, and I hadn't made time to talk to her, all wrapped up in my own misery, and not wanting anyone else to see. As if to grieve was a humiliation.

Was that enough to make her want to get at me so much? Maybe. She was slightly crazy.

More to the point, was her scheme working? I mean, was I scared?

I switched on the torch, then switched off the overhead

light. I left the torch burning by my bed. I lay down, listening, and heard only the vague sounds of wood and plaster settling towards the cool of earliest morning.

Yes, I was, if not nervous, unnerved.

I didn't think I could sleep. Then I did. I dreamed, of course. Not about the Woman in Yellow. I was meeting Eden at Heathrow to fly to the U.S. with him, and I was very happy about this, and then I found my passport had vanished, but there was my father, grey and old, saying "I've got it here, Laura. It's all right." But we looked through the window of the caravan, which was suddenly there, and in which (in the dream) he'd been living, and it was full of *things* – *live* things – not really mice, more like ghastly little gingerbread figures – and they were eating the furniture –

And I woke up with my heart in my mouth, and it was light, 6 a.m., and the clock was striking ten.

III

I left the next morning.

Let me rephrase that. I tried to leave.

Having got up and dressed and herded my bags together, I bundled everything down the main stair to the hall.

It was by then only six-twenty, and there was no sign of Jennifer. Though I suspected she was an early riser, it seemed not *this* early.

My plan was to use the phone I'd noted yesterday in the drawing-room, and call the remembered number of the cab firm who'd brought me here.

When I walked into the room, the sunlight was cutting through it from the east-facing windows, and I could see the ocean glittering away below, never now to be reached. But when I lifted the old-fashioned receiver of the telephone, there was no dialling tone. I tried various things, nothing worked. I thought perhaps Jennifer unplugged the phone at night, and traced the wire around to its socket in the wall. But it was attached, and although I took it out and reconnected it, still the phone was dead.

Probably the machine itself had gone wrong and she frugally hadn't bothered to get it mended. Where then in the house would I find another phone that worked?

I searched the downstairs rooms, cursing myself now that I, abnormality among millions, had never invested in one of those mobiles I'd previously cursed on the train. Of course the one I'd used from the company had been recalled.

The rooms were all spacious, gracious, full of grand furniture and silk curtains, and all soiled and dusty and lit by sun. And phoneless.

I went to the kitchen then and made myself some of the foul coffee, double strength. Really I thought I knew where the one operational phone would be. It would be in Jennifer's bedroom.

As I stood there, in that dampish, still, shadowy, stone-floored vault, my body was prickling all over finally with a kind of fear. I *knew* I couldn't say to her, I am leaving now: Let me use the phone to call a cab.

She would somehow (how?) prevent it.

She wanted me here, she really did. To play with, to get back at for imagined trespasses. And did she hope for me something worse than humiliation and housework?

Jennifer and Eugenia – just how much, by now, did the two of them have in common?

Then I visualised lugging my bags through the winding twisty lanes, getting lost among fields and hedges, always glimpsing the sea and the way I should go, and not able to figure out physically how to get there. I thought of surly country folk, who would detest me and refuse me use of *their* phones, snarling dogs, bulls – the perfect layman's picture of the English Wild. Whatever else, it would be a long walk. It had taken the cab nearly an hour...

So I thought of a cunning plot. I'm a sort of survivalist. Up to a point, I'll do what I have to, to escape, evade, get by.

She came down at eight. By then I was cleaning the French windows of the drawing-room. The rest of the room was dusted and hoovered, though not polished. You don't, even if on an economy drive, polish wood like that with *Busy Bee* – which was all she had.

I heard her stop in the doorway. Was she thrilled? Triumphant? Or at all startled I'd actually given in?

"Hi," I said airily, only half turning. "Beautiful morning."

"Yes, it is," she said, grudgingly.

"I've almost done in here. I thought you'd like this room sorted out first."

"Yes." Then she said, "So you decided you'd do it."

"Oh, why not?" I said. "For a while, anyway. It's a great house, it's good to tidy it up." Then I turned round properly. There she was, in a rather grubby white wrap, with her dyed hair in curlers and a scarf. I said, "Just one thing, I'm really sorry. When I was hoovering, I knocked into that table with the phone and it fell off. When I picked it up I couldn't get the tone. I must have broken it. Of course, I'll pay for the repair."

She blinked. That was all. Then her dire little smile came out like a hiding slug. "That's all right, Laura. It doesn't work anyway. I don't use the telephone much."

I gawped, *astonished,* and anxiously said, "But miles up here, and you live alone – do you keep another phone for emergencies at least?"

"Oh yes."

That was all. I turned back as if completely satisfied. Whistling, I went on sparkling up the windows with newspaper. I *was* satisfied. She did have another phone. Just a matter of finding it.

Then, as I gave the last burnish to the panes, I saw in the glass that Jennifer was now advancing through the room towards me, and – well, this frightened me. Was she violent? For a second I pretended to go on obliviously rubbing the newspaper about, but keeping my eyes on her reflection. The image was virtually divided between outside and in, and she seemed to be passing through the cedar tree in sections, her stupid red scarf, wound over curlers, very vivid in the glass, and contrastingly, her wrapper looking rather like a long dress, and more yellow than white –

And then I knew what I was seeing.

It wasn't my Aunt Jennifer.

I whirled round, burning cold, in a terror the like of which I'd never ever felt – a sort of vertigo of fear. As if a hole had opened in the world and I was about to plunge through.

Nothing was in the room.

Not Jennifer. Nothing... else.

I made a noise, a silly noise.

After quite some time, I looked back at the window, and there was only the vague reflection of furniture held there among the branches of the cedar.

What do you do after something like that? If you're me, and you don't believe in ghosts, fairly quickly you put it down to hallucination caused by stress. And then you feel slightly better.

However, I was all the more keen to get out of the house.

She wanted breakfast, of course. Toast, cornflakes, marmalade – and tea, *not* coffee. I prepared that and she had it in the drawing-room, taking the opportunity, as she did so, to write down on a note-pad anything she thought I'd missed in my cleaning.

After all that, I explained I was just popping up to the loo. I guessed I'd get some comment about weak bladders or irregular bowels, but no.

Upstairs I went, but obviously not to the bathroom. I walked along the main upper hallway, and looked into the rooms until I found hers.

Her room was disgusting.

I have lived, I've said, in tips, but she really had no excuse. The bed was tightly made, otherwise there was mess and junk everywhere, old newspapers in stacks, magazines, boxes of sticky old orange powder and make-up dried in tubes. And worse than this, half-eaten packets of biscuits, sweets that *seemed* half-eaten, then taken out and *wrapped up again in their paper for future use* – Another defunct banana lay rotting in a turpentine reek on the windowsill, to the glee of several flies. The room stank of that, of many saccharine things going off. Of her.

I opened windows, and then I looked for the phone. And it wasn't there. Which was insane, for it was nowhere else and I truly didn't believe even crazy Jennifer wouldn't have one. She must have concealed it cleverly. Where?

Perhaps I was chicken, I didn't want to start rummaging around yet. I'd have to tell her I would do her room this afternoon, make it nice for her, some crap like that.

Then I went down to get on with the drudgery, and unlike me, *she* had found something – my bags, thrust in the hall cupboard.

"Whatever are these doing here? I said take them up."

"Oh, I will, when I sort them out later. They take up too much space in my room like this."

I can sometimes think on my feet.

But perhaps I wasn't fooling her. Had she been looking?

A curious day. I laboured like her slave. My arms began to ache, and my back from bending and stretching. With the mirrors and the windows, I whistled and sang Mozart and XTC extra loud, and saw nothing beyond what usually reflects in glass.

I made lunch, (canned pilchards), and ate some with her.

The pilchards seemed to give her a high. She started rambling on at me. I scarcely listened to her reminiscences – everything had been much better then, maybe for her it had – and diatribes against men in general, Lesbians in particular, the French, the Germans, the Americans, the Scottish, and those she chose to call "Negroes" (!), also workmen, all of them, and the money-grabbing, work-shy, n'ere-do-wells who had ruined the British economy, and perhaps included, unspoken, me.

I wanted to kill her. It's a fact. I felt I too was going mental. Didn't care what I might come to do.

Acting Oscar-earning well, I smarmily told her I'd decided to clean her bedroom.

"No, Laura, that can wait. There's still plenty to see to on this floor."

"Okay," I said.

Sod her. She wasn't going to stop me now.

The old witch had a rest after lunch, so she had told me, but not in her bedroom, in one of the downstairs rooms.

To this stroke of luck I replied I'd clean up in the kitchen, while she slept, so as not to disturb her.

"Oh, I don't sleep, Laura. I never sleep well."

"Just in case," Laura cheerily declared.

As I cleared the lunch things and went out, she was smiling to herself, a crafty slug smile. But this had gone far enough, and I meant to be out of this appalling house before nightfall. Even if I did have to walk all the way with my bags gripped in my teeth, and sleep on the beach when I got there.

Accordingly, all that afternoon I searched, mainly on the upper floor. I even got up into the attics by another narrow back stair – but they were such a shambles, and draped so thickly with cobwebs, I thought perhaps she hadn't herself gone up there in a decade. I didn't find a phone. I began to feel she had lied when she said she had another, just to get me running in circles. (Somehow, during all this circle-running, I'd managed to avoid going anywhere near the clock. I'd even used the other bathroom.)

The hot afternoon light was abruptly slanting. It was nearly five.

There she was, standing in the lower hall, glaring up at me.

"Why ever are you up there? I expected tea an hour ago."

"Sorry, I'll get it now," I heard myself say, still with vague self-amazement.

"I told you not to clean upstairs yet."

"I haven't. Sorry," I said again, "I took a nap."

Firmly I added, "I didn't have a great night."

She shrugged – placated? "Very well. We'll let it go. See to the tea now."

So I saw to the tea.

Inside me at last was a mindless – almost bestial – rising panic. I couldn't seem to pull myself around. I couldn't seem to confront her any more, or make up my mind what it was best for me to do. And in about three hours, the sun was going down, down into the land, leaving behind a darkness that would smother even that coal-blue sea, which looked as if it belonged in Africa, but had somehow washed up here. As had I, who might also – be smothered?

In the end what I did was drag all my bags down to the kitchen, (having found another way on to the back stair from the ground floor; I wouldn't return to my 'room' – or just wouldn't go by the clock.) In the kitchen, I sorted through them in the mode of life-boat intendees in movies. I was going to have to leave a lot behind; it would be too heavy to carry all that way.

At the finish, I had it all down to one single very heavy bag. This I then picked up, and walked upstairs again, as I hadn't been able to open the kitchen door to the outside, it was stuck – or locked.

In the lower hall, once more, I met her. She'd known, she must have done, all of it, even to my breaking point.

But "What are you doing, Laura?" she asked. She had put on lipstick, as if for a celebration.

I moved across, and paused facing her, at the foot of the main stair. She was between me and the front door. I put down my bag. I felt reckless.

"Sorry," I said again, "I just remembered I left the kettle on in London."

"You're leaving after all," she brilliantly fathomed.

"Sure am. I don't suppose you'll allow me to use the secret

telephone to call a cab?"

"Certainly not, at this time of night," (it was about seven). "They wouldn't come out. Not all the way up here. If you really insist on going, then you must do it in the morning."

"No. I'm not spending another night here. Not with you, or your speciality ghosts."

She smiled. What a giveaway.

"Don't tell me a grown-up woman, even you, is frightened by a ghost story."

"I don't give a toss about ghost stories. I just don't like *you*, Aunt Jennifer, or your behaviour."

"It's mutual, then," she said. We stood there in the cup of the brown hall, dusted by me, and the tiled floor wiped to a gleam, as sunlight speared by in its death-throes. "Oh, don't think I ever could forget the way you used to behave to me. You, a child. I used to think she put you up to it, that slut of a mother of yours. But I don't think she would have bothered. She'd got *him* where she wanted him. And she was busy making a fool of him. She killed him with her goings-on."

"Shut up," I said, but almost listlessly, because I half agreed at least on that. She didn't take any notice anyway.

"But you were a dreadful little girl. I always saw you sneering at me behind my back, laughing at me. Always trying to get me to buy you things –"

"For God's sake I was a child –"

"She'd told you I was well-off, I suppose. And so it was: Can I have an ice-cream, can I go to the pictures, can I have that book on tigers –?"

"Well I didn't get them off you, did I? Oh, excuse me, I did get half an ice-cream once."

She shamed me. Had I been a whining, gift-grabbing kid? We hadn't had much, and Jennifer, then, used to flash her money. And she used to promise me things, too, presents, and at first I'd believed her, but I never got them. In me now, the panic was boiling into rage. The hall was stifling and turning red with it. Like her furious self-righteous face.

"Then the funeral," she announced. "My own brother, and your father, and there you were, and you couldn't say a word to me, just 'Hallo, Aunt'. And later I think you said good-bye. Both of us standing there over his grave, and you wouldn't say a word. You couldn't even spare me a drop of kindness."

"My father was dead," I said bitterly.

"My *brother* was dead," she cried. Her eyes flamed like slices of razor, and then they went up over my head, up to the top of the stairs, and she let out – not a scream – a sort of yelp.

At once the blood-red light in the hall seemed to darken. Something out there had got hold of the sun. Instantly, the nature of my turmoil changed. My back, my neck, my scalp, were covered by freezing ants.

I stared at her. "What is it?"

She didn't speak. She simply went on gazing up the stairway, and, still gazing, she began to back away, back through the door of the drawing-room, and now her lipstick mouth was hanging open.

I've no notion how, but I understood this was not part of the game.

As for me, for a moment I didn't think I *could* move. Then I knew I had to, because otherwise, if I just stayed there at the foot of the stairs, whatever – whatever was on them, coming down them, whatever that was – would soon be right where *I* was – and I didn't – no I *didn't* – want that –

So I somehow moved forward, to run after Jennifer through the drawing-room door, and at the same time, like Lot's misguided wife, I looked behind me –

And was turned, as she was, to an immovable pillar of volcanic salt.

Because what was standing still at the head of the stairs was the wooden clock, and what was coming *down* the stairs was Sabia Trente, not still at all, the skirts of her gown blowing round her, and her arms held up from the elbows, and her hands pointing with their grown-long finger-nails –

You see such things on a screen, a book-jacket, on the

bloody Internet for God's sake, such images of gothic horror, these evocations of dynamic terror. It doesn't prepare you for the actual thing.

There she was. And she was worse than anything anyone could ever physically mock up, or imagine.

Her face was white, blue-white, and marked by the fringe of blood that was still unravelling down her right cheek, and yet never reached her already blood-stained gown or the stairs. Her forehead was red and also bruised black, and quills of bone stood out of her hair, (like a Spanish comb), which was otherwise clotted scarlet with blood. Her face had features, all sunken in and withered. It was a fallen monkey's face, yet too, like a mask – and in the place where her eyes had once been – were only two bruised black sockets of nothing, each secured in her head by a shining silver pin –

All I wanted was to run. It was the sum of my ambitions. And I couldn't do it. Could not move.

And so Sabia Trente came down the stair, and right up to me, and I smelled her stink worse than dead rats or rotting bananas, and then she passed directly through me, like a dank, dust-laden wind.

Perhaps I died for a split second when that happened. Perhaps my heart stopped. I don't know, can't remember.

It was just that suddenly she was past me, and I was still rooted there, watching her glide, as if she moved on ice-skates over a rink, through the drawing-room door.

Darkness had come, premature night. Once before I'd seen this creature move across the room, seen her in the window. Now I saw her from the back. Saw her so clearly, *solidly*, even the creases of her dress and the bones of her corset under it.

And I saw my Aunt Jennifer too, sprawled on a brocade sofa, screaming now, shrieking, and trying to bury her head in the cushions.

On which cue, Sabia Trente was raising up high a kind of stick, an iron thing like a wand with a strange glowing tip – she hadn't had it a moment ago – and I knew it was the poker from a fire that had been out for more than a century.

She was going to return the compliment of the cloven braincase, not on her murderous, no longer available Aunt Eugenia, but on the skull of Jennifer.

I told you from the start, I don't believe in ghosts. I don't. I flatly refuse to. If I did, I think I would lose my mind for sure and for real and for good. And so, in those moments that lingered between Jennifer and me and the gates of Hell, I saw it all, what had truly happened, and *why* this thing was here, and what it was and what to do about it.

I was numb, had no feeling in my body, didn't really seem to be *in* it, except perhaps sitting tiny and high up behind my own eyes, like a lone passenger left on a train hurtling driverless to destruction.

For the train – me, driverless – was all at once rushing forward. It crashed headlong into the back of the stationary Sabia - I *felt* her – and I tore her apart with my hands, screaming myself now, over and over, "Go away – get lost – piss off – you don't exist –"

And she didn't exist. She was only air, and then she and her poker were gone. And at the head of the stairs the clock became a black cloud and then was gone too, back to its place in reality along the corridor.

I stood over Jennifer and I bawled at her now, "You made it up, didn't you, you fucking old bitch – *didn't* you?"

She whimpered. I struck her across the head. Not so hard. It was much better than a poker would have been. Then I pulled her to a sitting position and shouted abuse at her until she spoke. "I didn't – it was true – or at least in the book. Only not – not –"

"Not what, you cow?"

"Not that clock. Not *that* one."

She had wanted to pay me out for all my seven, nine and twenty-year-old transgressions against her. So she never quite lost track of me, and when the company folded, she was ready.

Yes, I was to have been her skivvy. For I must be punished. And, muddled as Jennifer had become, she had invested in the invented memory of me as a sensitive, nervy girl, ready to be dominated and scared witless by a contrived ghost story.

Although, as she'd said, the story was true – at least in a bona fide book, which carried the tale of the Trente murder and the haunted French clock. Even the piece about Shelley Terrence, though he had never lived in Jennifer's house – all these events had gone on somewhere else. For that reason she had had to copy out all the passages. To photocopy the printed text would have revealed too much and given the game away.

She had read the story one idle afternoon. And become obsessed enough to weave it into her retribution for me. And so mad, mad Aunt Jennifer, who wouldn't even pay to have her downstairs telephone repaired, forked out quite a sum to gain a rather poor reproduction of the Trente clock. This copy it was which was then placed – *unnailed* – in the corridor by my elected bedroom. She had even arranged for its random striking.

Well, she was off her head. And her loathing insanity and my allergic anger seem to have been enough. For yes, I take part of the blame. Without my side of it, I don't think it would have happened; she couldn't have done it on her own.

And what did happen?

Neither Jennifer nor I had ever had a child – in my case from choice, in hers I don't know. But we made a type of child between us, an *offspring* in that word's purest and most dreadful sense. For we fashioned the ghost of Sabia Trente between us, brought it to its unlife, and made it *run*.

If simply that, our projected hating energy, would have been sufficient to make the vengeful poker and its blow fatal – I've got no idea. Maybe. After all, I stopped it. I must have thought so then.

But, too, perhaps Jennifer and I merely hallucinated – visions of similar aspect experienced by more than one person at once, aren't uncommon in the annals either of the supernatural or science.

Whatever, as I said, this wasn't a ghost story, although it has a ghost.

And what happened *afterwards*? Soon told. She did a lot of cringing and crying her dry hard tears. But now I managed to make it clear I wouldn't stay another hour in her house.

I waited outside for the taxi, which took me away fast, so I just caught the nine-thirty-five train to London. The phone? I hardly believe it myself – she, the arch-reviler of modernity, had a weeny little mobile tucked in her handbag.

As I was going out of her door she came scurrying at me from the now thick-lit shadows of the house, and pushed a paper bag into my hand. I thought it probably contained some stale sandwiches to give me indigestion, or some already half-eaten sweets. I wanted to slap it to the ground, but something made me take it. Otherwise we parted without a touch, or another word. I didn't look at the paper bag until the train was drawing into London and I was going to throw it away.

Inside was a hundred pounds in tens, and a cheque for three thousand pounds. This was so obscene I felt nauseous. Or maybe that was only hunger, and the shock from everything else. I didn't throw up. I did cash and spend the money. And what does that make me?

I'm wondering though, if you wonder... if, despite the clock's being only a copy - yet somehow it did draw back the vengeance-seeking Sabia's dead remnant – and only my vaunted stupidity drove her off. No. However, your choice. Somebody said, it wasn't the dead you need to fear, but the living. Too damn right.

Since that night, I've heard nothing more from Jennifer. Years have elapsed. Now and then I ask myself what she does, alone, when it gets dark in that house.

The Lady-of-Shalott House

A river like black glass ran by the place. Above, bone pale, stood the old house with its dark, sloped roofs. It had one of those towers, too, where a pair of windows face each other, so the light of the sky through one, shines out through the other, and this other window, looking down to the road, seemed even by day to have a lamp in it. All around went the hills, also pale and bleached by the sun. Trees grew on some with sombre leaves. And by the river grew strange huge marigolds – if they were – the colour of orange curd.

Carey Pearce, who had not yet become a well-known painter, paused on the road, staring across the river, up at the house, and the hills behind. He began memorising the scene for a canvas, especially the marigolds, which looked primal and nearly carnivorous.

It was late afternoon, and he was on his way to the home of distant cousins he had never met. The train ran only to the station he had left an hour before, and here the horse he had been promised was out on other business. Carrying his bag, therefore, he had started to walk. He found this a haphazard country, all told, but one he liked. He did not think he would reach the house of his cousins until evening.

Down in the valley to the south, he could see the black trail of the railway, and along it another toy train was just now puffing, its smoke-stack sending up a plume into the westering sun-ambered sky.

When Carey glanced back at the pale house, he saw a woman was seated on the veranda. And she had hair, he afterwards said, definitely the exact shade of the marigolds by the river.

He thought she had not been there before, but now she was. She looked at the road, or maybe at the train below. In any case, he raised his hat.

Her dress was dark, caught with a silver brooch at the throat. She was of that slim small type, and her face seemed an unusual one under the pile of remarkable hair.

Carey moved off the road, went over the river by a narrow bridge, brushed through the marigolds, and came up to a white-painted picket fence. Here he stood and gazed up, and the woman looked back at him.

"Can you tell me, am I on the right road for the Hannifer house?"

He realised then she had not been looking at him, or not truly, for now her eyes seemed to change. It was, he thought, as if a cloudy liquid grew suddenly clear.

"Oh, yes," she said. She had a sweet voice. He decided she might be able to sing well.

"I hope it's near. I've walked from the station, and it's a hot day."

All this was blatant deception. He knew perfectly well he was on the right road, and knew too he had another hour's walk at least before him. He was fit, his bag was light enough, and he was used to walking; he had climbed fells in England, and small Alps in France, from dawn to dusk, in search of images to paint.

What he wanted was that the woman with marigold hair would invite him to step up and sit with her. She was beautiful, and in an almost classical way. Just as he knew when he had found the view he wanted, so he knew he had found in her a portrait. No doubt there was a husband, even children, and probably servants, in the pale house. He must charm them all, and be asked back.

She did not speak at first, then she said, "It's a long way, I fear." She sounded remote, like a well-schooled infant that does not know the precise meaning of the lesson it has learned.

"Very long?" inquired Carey, putting a querulous note into his tone. "Oh, I was on that train for thirteen hours, cooked alive. They said I'd find a horse to ride at the station, but no such luck."

In the garden that climbed to the house, bushes of fiery flowers had run wild. A parrot tree stooped almost to the ground with unpicked fruit.

She said, "You must be tired."

But nothing else.

Then he looked more attentively at the house. The sun was on it, burning on the windows, just as the bright north sky burned through the window of the tower. But he seemed to see curtains drawn, or absent. The veranda was in want of repair. There was an old rocker in which she sat, and one other chair, a notable one with carved back and arms. A cane table had been set between, and he noticed now all at once it had a decanter on it and a crystal jug, and two tall glasses and two glasses for wine. But in the decanter and the jug and the glasses was nothing, nothing at all but a thick smoke of dust shining in the low sun.

Carey Pearce said, "I wonder if I might come up and sit with you for a few minutes. Forgive my boldness. Perhaps your husband –"

She said, "My brother has gone away. But come up if you want. I have nothing to offer you –" this struck him oddly, she did not say it in a churlish way – "but the river is very pure, if you wish to drink."

Carey took her at her word. He went down the bank, knelt, and cupped up in his hand a couple of mouthfuls of the black, bright, transparent water. It was clean and pleasant. But he had wanted to show her he was accepting her hospitality, such as it was.

Something must have happened here, some family matter. The brother gone away, the servants vanished.

He opened a little white gate in the picket fence, and went through. He went up the garden path under the parrot tree, and so the steps to the veranda. As he stood over her, she lifted her pale quiet face to his. His heart stopped a moment. She had that kind of loveliness which makes its subject seem known, as if we half recall something very beautiful from another time and place, for here is its reminder.

"I'm sorry to trouble you," he said.

"It's no trouble."

"My name is Carey Pearce," he said. "My cousins are the Hannifers, but we've never met. May I sit down?"

She looked at the other chair, and then back at him, and all at once she laughed. It was a soft melodious laugh, not exactly mocking – more playful. "Please do, Mr Pearce."

He sat. And there was another odd thing. The chair, though such a good one, felt extremely uncomfortable. He thought at first he was more travel-worn than he had believed; and serve him right for pretending to be so. Then he concluded that it was simply a badly-made chair, all show and no substance.

But he opened his bag and took out a bottle of fruit cordial.

"May I offer you some of this?"

"Oh no. Nothing, thank you."

"Then, do you object if I drink it alone?"

She said then, without the least sign or nuance of rudeness, "Don't use the glasses, Mr Pearce."

He supposed she was sensible of their dirtiness, so he nodded, and drank the cordial from the bottle.

Then she folded her hands in her lap and rested her wonderful head back on her chair, and she began gently to rock. She said not a word, yet it was not from shyness, he thought, nor coldness. It was as if she knew him well, and might be silent with him without offence.

He was used to silence himself, and unlike most people often alone, he rather liked it.

So he sat in the uncomfortable chair as comfortably as he could, which was not very, and looked down the hills to the valley and the snake coils of the train track, looked at the exotic sombre-leafed trees and the flames of the flowers. He listened to the hush of that wide, scorched land, broken only now and then by a daytime cricket, and once at the whistle of an unseen bird.

The sun slanted more and more to the west, and a line of clouds, a herd of them, tumbled slowly before it.

At intervals, he turned and studied the woman very carefully. She did not seem to mind this, if she was aware of it at all. Throughout his life Carey had had the knack of making a mental sketch, for he had begun early to want sometimes to create pictures of things and spots where sketching on paper was either inadvisable or frankly impossible. But he drew the lines of the woman's face over and over in his mind, cautiously etched in the translucent first shadows, and the dilute clear amber of the light – and the wash of hair that would be so easy to paint with some splash of colour direct from a tube, which meant he must be more subtle and try to capture it another way.

She was about twenty-five, he thought, not quite young, but not turned either, as women often did in this climate, to that dryness and toughness of skin the critic termed *leathering*. Her eyes were grey-azure, opaque yet glimmering as moonstones. If he could reproduce that, and the angle of her brows, the lilt of her throat with the small winking brooch at its nadir, he would have something very fine.

The sun was now into the clouds, herding them down beyond the valley. A certain alteration of blueness was at the core of the sky. The day was working toward sunset.

He said, rather low, not to break her reverie harshly, "It's late. I'd better be getting on. Thank you for your oasis."

She did not look at him now. Her eyes were back on the road. She said, "Go safely."

"You're kind. I will. And you."

"Oh, I am safe enough," she said.

But when he was out of the awful chair and standing, a compunction seized him as if he had only just become aware of things.

"Are you quite alone here? Is everything all right with you? Shall I –?"

"Everything's well," she said.

That was all.

But when he gazed down at her, she was smiling. He thought she seemed happy and at ease. And so he only offered another farewell and left her, walking down through the garden, and closing the gate with elaborate care.

Once over the river and on the road, he turned again to signal goodbye, but the sun had reached just that point to dazzle away the images of the veranda. Indeed, the whole building appeared curiously to float like a bubble, suspended in the air. He could not make her out at all, and perhaps anyway she had now gone inside.

Carey reached the Hannifer house in the last of the dusk. He was struck at once by its bustle and life. Kerosene lamps hung along the veranda, every window was lit behind its lace rosy yellow, and men and horses came and went through the pastures behind.

Soon enough all the cousins swelled out in a swarm. His hand was wrung, a large beaming woman embraced him. He was led into a parlour with a rose lamp in its window, and presently into supper under a chandelier, with two rough and massive dogs lying for contrast by the hearth.

They were as hungry for his stories of the world as any people he had ever come across. He had to tell them anecdotes of a ship in Africa, and of a French village, and even about the great city he had just left, which most of them had never seen. Between whiles they poured him wine, and loaded his plate of pleasing brown and white china with potatoes, vegetables, pie and relishes. Afterwards there was a lemon dessert, and cigarettes and brandy were brought, and he sat alone with the men in an up-country English sort of way, hearing the women's bright laughter in another room.

All this time there had been no opening to speak of anything close to home. Even the omission of the station horse they had swept quickly away with an, "Of all the lousy shows!" But as he and the men now lounged, with the veranda doors wide, and the crickets sounding in their silver night chorus, counterpart to the croak of frogs in the swamp beyond the river, Carey turned to his new cousin, Joseph.

"Before I reached your house, there was another. Just off the road. About three, four miles back. A white house, with a tower."

Joseph Hannifer nodded idly enough. "Yes, that's the Collins place. Run down now."

"I thought I might paint it," said Carey. It was as if something whispered to him, the crickets perhaps, that he must beware what he said. "Who lives there?"

"No one at present. It was Tappy Collins' place, but he moved away years ago."

"Tappy Collins? Now the man at the station mentioned him, I think," lied Carey nimbly, sipping his brandy. A great moth, large as a dollar bill, had come from the night and hovered over the veranda rail above the lamps. The flicker of its wings was like one more warning. "The man said Collins had a sister – or do I have it wrong?"

"Old Ned's a rare old gossip. Right enough, Tappy had a sister."

Carey waited, and as he did, considered the tense of the word *had*.

"Had he? I thought –"

"Oh, it's a sad story. A bad story."

Old Uncle Someone – Carey did not yet grasp all the names – had fallen asleep. Two male cousins mildly joked about this. Two others had gone out to see to something in the outbuildings and stables, the dogs padding after them.

From the women's parlour winged up more laughter, and the notes of a tinny but game piano.

"Can I know the tale?" asked Carey.

"We're not proud of it," said Joseph. "But there. You'll make a painting of it, maybe." And Carey was alerted to the first hint of acrimony in Joseph Hannifer, his cousin.

Then Joseph told him the story, and the other men were,

mostly silent, but for the mild-snoring uncle. Now and then, one added something. They shook their heads. The room was warm, and smoky from the pipes, and outside stood the black walls of the night, into which the giant moth flew away.

Tappy Collins had had the house from his father. The mother was long dead, though it was she had given the property its queer and fanciful name. It was the title of some poet's poem – Carey forbore to speak the other name of Tennyson – a crazy notion that was talked about.

Lady-of-Shalott the house was called, after this ballad about a damsel who drowned herself. And Carey forbore to correct them, since the Lady of Shalott had not drowned but only lain down in a magic boat and died of love.

"Well Tappy kept his sister – Maudra, the mother had called her – to look after the house, and it was a downright waste of her. She was a pretty thing, but day-dreamy – perhaps too much that way for some. But she could have made a marriage, no doubt of that. Tappy, though, he shut her up at home, and she never saw another soul but him and the maids. They said he promised her, 'When I get wed then you can do as you like'. But perhaps he never said that."

"The man at the station – Ned – told me she had strange-coloured hair."

"Orange," said Joseph, and one of the other cousins added, "Yes, Orange as marmalade. But apart from that, she had good looks."

Joseph continued. He said that a day came when a man rode out to the house on business with Tappy Collins, and he took one look at Maudra and wanted her, body and soul. And it was the same with her.

"Trouble was," said Joseph, "the fellow was married already, hard and fast, and no getting out of it."

Carey listened, until the cigarette burned his fingers and the men laughed slyly at him. But his hands were as hard from paint as theirs from manual work, and he did not mind.

He was seeing Maudra and her dreaming eyes, seeing her in

love. The man they did not much describe – he had a shock of thick blond hair, enough to turn any silly woman's head. Enough money as well to dress elegantly and smell of cologne. Edmund Dyle was his name.

"Well, he had his way with her. Tappy was off in the city, and they used his house to their own advantage."

"I heard," said another cousin, "they lay down in every room."

Joseph said, "You've got a course tongue, Matt. But so they did, probably."

"What happened then?" said Carey softly.

"Once he'd had his fill, Dyle ran back to his wife," said Joseph. His was, thought Carey, a cruel voice, judgmental and now slightly shrill.

Carey no longer liked Joseph. He said nothing.

Joseph said, "He's stayed with the wife, too, though off and on he has another fling with some girl or other, with her head on backwards and not got the sense she was born with."

The cousin who had also spoken said, "But Maudra died."

Carey breathed out a long sigh. "Did she?"

"Died of a broken heart," said the other cousin.

"Poor little thing. She was twenty-five years old."

"She took a fever," said Joseph. "Brain fever. That was how she died. There was a story she drowned herself like the girl in the ballad. But she didn't."

Yet, Carey Pearce thought, Maudra had died rather in the way of the Lady of Shalott after all, if she had died of love, breaking her imprisonment. He said, after a moment, lighting a cigarette, attending the advice of the cautioning crickets, "Ned told me there was some idea the house was haunted. Now I see why."

"Tappy went off soon enough," said Joseph. "But Tappy was a fool."

The Hannifer uncle had woken. He spoke without emphasis. "Two or three persons have seen Maudra Collins sitting on her veranda, since her death, in the old rocker. She looks out to the road." He seemed to watch Carey acutely; maybe it was only the light on his spectacles. "If you wave, she may wave back to you. She's a polite little creature still."

Carey said, "How long ago did she die? Was it recent?"

"Fifteen years," said the uncle. "Sixteen, next March."

Later, Carey climbed the stairs and found a milk-white bedroom, washed himself, and got into bed. He blew out the lamp; there was no gas here, let alone electricity.

In the night peculiar sounds came from the hills beyond the house of the Hannifers. Carey knew, from all the alien nights he had slept and lain through, in russet little rooms up under thatch, in barns and empty styes, in the wide chambers of hollow, dark hotels, where golden beetles ran about the floors, that the noises of unknown night are always uncanny. He was not alarmed. Nor did the ghost of Maudra dismay him. He had been privileged to get so much more than a wave, to come so close. And he was glad she had not seemed afraid or sad, or shown any vestige of her pitiful, lonely unloved death. She was peaceful now, hopeful almost. Yes, he was glad.

The next day Joseph Hannifer wanted to ride with his Cousin Carey to the town, ten miles east. The women cousins protested that Carey was too tired, but Carey was not tired, and he was intrigued by Joseph, even not liking Joseph, because Joseph had mostly told him the story of Maudra Collins.

They started early enough, and the sun was white, and the sky that unique brazen sheet that is not blue at all, and the parched hills rolled round them, with their tufts of trees, and the occasional groves of farms, and the woods, and the swampland with its spears of razorous grass and muggy lilies. The horses were strong and courteous. But Cousin Joseph still kept expecting Carey Pearce to make some mistake. When a rabbit bolted across the road, for example, Joseph looked at Carey, all crinkled up in the face, to see the horse shy and throw him. But Carey and the horse were quite calm. Joseph seemed to have made up his mind that a man who painted pictures would be able to do nothing else. Soon Joseph began to talk about illnesses of the region, brainstorms and ailments of the bowel from poisoned water, and about renegades and thieves. All this, it seemed, to see if Carey would get nervous. But Carey only listened and asked reasonable questions.

They were about four miles from the town when Joseph said, almost violently, "Why, see that fellow walking down there, on the road?"

"Yes, I do."

"See his hair?"

Carey looked more fully, and saw the man was flaxen fair, which was not very uncommon here.

Joseph said, "From the style of him, he goes on like that wretch I told you of, Edmund Dyle, Maudra's fancy. Only I'd expect him to be riding."

The sun was going over from the zenith, and it shone from behind them all down the road, and made it, but for their shadows, white and polished as glass. The man appeared half there and half not in this devouring light. He came on at a steady pace, striding west as they rode east, to meet them.

"Edmund Dyle," said Joseph. "It could be. Maybe that rich wife of his got sick of his escapades and threw him out at last."

They rode on, and the man who might be Edmund Dyle drew closer. Carey was interested. He wanted to gaze into the face of Maudra's betrayer, wanted to scan it for future use on canvas. Judas has always been of artistic value, in whatever form.

Even so, Carey felt a little ashamed. Because he thought he understood already that something of Maudra was drawing Edmund Dyle, if so the man was, drawing him to her despite himself. For him she watched the road. For him the best chair waited, unwelcoming of any other – and for him it would be comfortable. And the decanter and the crystal jug would sparkle full of wine and lemonade.

The countryside was empty here, excepting the stands of umbrous trees. Soon enough they came up with the walking man, and when they were some thirty feet from him, Joseph swore. "It's him. I tell you," he added, as if Carey had argued, "it's Dyle."

Joseph reigned in. And so Carey copied him.

"Hey, Dyle! Is it you?"

The walker came on, then stopped. He was near. He looked up at Joseph's face, and as if finding the paucity of it, his eyes continued until they found Carey.

"Sir," said the man on the road, "I've lost my way. I used to know these parts, and yet... I'm searching for the Collins house."

Joseph vented another curse. But along Carey Pearce's spine there moved upwards a pale, quiet, electric tremor, as when grass turns before the wind and whitens.

"Follow the road," said Carey. "Just follow the road and you'll come to it. But it's a long way."

"Yes, a long way," said Edmund Dyle. "But I've come a long way already."

Carey meant to say something else, but the words stuck in his mouth. Then, as the man walked by him in his elegant dusty coat, he found to his surprise he said, "God bless you. God bless you both."

Joseph sat his horse, snorted, and kicked its shanks. They rode on again.

"He's gone daft," said Joseph. "It was him, all right, but addled. His tie was all undone. His gloves were stained. And that's no coat to go trekking in."

Carey glanced back. He watched Edmund Dyle walk west along the road, the white sun blazing above and before him. But when Joseph half turned and said angrily, "What's up now?" Carey only answered, "Nothing."

"Is he still there, the idiot?"

"No." To deflect Joseph, Carey lied. "I think he's gone off the road into the trees."

"Good riddance," said Joseph. His face bulged now with malevolence and scorn, and for a while, though never looking

The Lady-of-Shalott House

back as Carey Pearce had done, Joseph Hannifer railed against the Dyles, all of them.

But when they came to the town and went into a bar there, he had to alter his tune.

So Joseph got drunk, until he had to hurry into the yard, and Carey held his shoulders as he threw up, and then supported Joseph when he sank down.

"We never met that bastard," said Joseph, through his fits of shaking. "Never. Not us. For Christ's sake," said Joseph, as though they had committed a crime on the road, "don't tell a soul we met him."

For Edmund Dyle had, the previous evening, shot himself point blank through the heart and dropped dead in his wife's fine house. He left a letter, which was now common property, that is, what it said, for he told her he had only ever loved one, and that one not her, but Maudra Collins who had died because of him.

Fifteen years and more the worm of regret had gnawed through Edmund Dyle, and in the end, to stop the pain, he had fired into himself the worst pain of all, which ends all others.

At sundown, Joseph begged Carey that he would not speak of any of this to the family in the Hannifer house, and Carey agreed to be silent.

But in the end, Carey Pearce was not silent at all, for he painted those two pictures, which anyone may see, where they hang in the gallery, or in reproduction. And the pictures speak loudly enough.

The first is the landscape with figure, which he called *The Lady-of-Shalott House*, a rich study of terrain, but mostly of a girl with extraordinary hair, seated in a rocking chair on a veranda, above the wild garden, and the black river with marigolds.

The second picture is more simple, and stranger. This is called only *Going Home*.

It shows a sun-blasted track, which carves between pale hills, and on the track a man, walking away, his back turned to the onlooker.

It is either the worm of regret, or the bullet of a pistol, which has cut right through him, showing what Carey Pearce saw so clearly on the road: how the sun shines straight as a spear through Edmund Dyle's body, at the area of the heart, forming one blinding ray of otherwise inexplicable light.

The Minstrel's Tale

It's true, I live by the making of songs, and of stories, too. And sometimes by the making of a fine good lie. But this is none of those, and so I swear, by any saint or angel that was ever kind to me. It happened not long ago, a little less than a year, and stays clear in my mind, though I'm thinking it will stay clear as the rich glass in a lord's church window, till my death day. Certainly, I'm a young man, and a year younger then, a vagabond, a trickster, though never yet, by God, a thief. But in the end, youth and honesty and trade make small odds. Listen, and judge for yourselves.

I'd sung a well-paid month in a town, for the castle folk and the plump folk in the houses, and I'd had my stomach full of that, and come walking away up into the heart of the land, to sing in the villages and the inns, where you get a pot of ale and a kiss for your work, and the sweeter for that, sometimes. Here was a place I'd never journeyed before, the country they call Dark Hills. And well named, its deep curved shoulders sombre as old smoke at their tops, brown and green as baked apple at their bases. While, in the long shining gloaming of the North, each peak and valley seems to swim away, growing ever farther off, like rings spreading in a pool after the flint is thrown in it, and I that flint.

In such a gloaming, between such hills, I passed a well. A may tree grew there, snowed with blossom, and below I saw the little stone cot with its stone-piled wall, and some tangled sheep sat cat-fashion, with their legs tucked under, on the slope above.

Now it's a fact, no matter how long the twilight, it must end in a night. I had been thinking of a grass bed, and still thought of it, for not every wayside dwelling welcomes a fellow with a harp on his back. But I went to the door and knocked.

Vapour came from the chimney, which was not much more than a central hole, the old way, such as you find here. But being at home was no promise of admitting another. Then the door was opened, and a man stood before me.

I've heard it said: The shepherd resembles his flock, and surely this one did. His face was dark and long, his eyes black, his long nose in the flattened Roman manner. His beard and hair might well have been a grizzled fleece. His hands and feet were tapering and miniature. To have him greet me on all fours would not have amazed me, nor to hear him go "baaa". But instead he looked in my face and he said to me: "Aye?"

"God's evening to you," I replied. "My trade is harping and songs, but I lack shelter. Can we bargain on that, or shall I be off?"

He went on looking me over, and I looked at him in a way I've learned. Sometimes you must offer more than songs in the back hills, or seem to offer more.

At length he nodded. He put on a prideful foolish smile and stood to one side, waving me to enter, which is an antique courtesy to the stranger. I thanked him, and ducked under the low lintel and went in.

It was dim inside, with smoke and dusk. There was the cooking place and the fire of peats, the black rafters, a great chest with some tools laid by on it. A ladder went up at one corner to a half room above. The bed-chamber that would be, for in winter the flock must cram in here with the master. We sat down on sheepskins, and he indicated the iron pot set to bubble over the peat.

"There's enough for all," he said. "When Rosemay comes, she'll give us ale."

This did surprise me, I was not sure quite why, that he should have a woman to tend him. Somehow he seemed a solitary creature, and his house had a bachelor's air to it, though tidy, no female thing scattered, and no carding comb or spinning wheel, but they would be above, perhaps.

"Your wife's from home?" I said. It might, after all, be a

The Minstel's Tale

daughter; it was as well to know.

"My wife," he said. "Did you not spy her at the well?"

I remembered the well and the snowy may tree growing there. I had seen no one, or I would have offered to draw the water for her, or carry the jar. By such ingratiating ploys one sometimes earns one's lodging. But his tone was humorous, as if this were some jest.

"No, I did not."

"Well, no grief. For here she is."

So I looked up, as he did, and through the opened door, the earthen jar in her hand, stepped his wife, his Rosemay.

I have been about, and I've beheld a woman or two was worth gazing at, and some indeed have been more than sisters to me. But this one. No, I had seen none like her.

The grey-mauve sky was behind her, the dark fireglow before, and she was a note of light between, tawny light, like certain wines I've seen, or candleflame. Her gown was yellow, a holy-day gown, too fine to fetch water or cook supper in, yet she wore it. Her hair was paler yellow than the gown, all loose, save for the two braids that held the sidelocks off her face and bound them up on her crown with a silk ribbon no different in colour than her hair. Her face and throat and hands were kissed all over by the summer sun. The lords' women keep themselves white, like milk, but this maid was ivory and cream and rose. Yes, a yellow rose she was, and with the beauty of a rose.

Then she stepped into the house, and darkened with its shadow to a rose of swarthy gold.

And here I was, about to be in his debt for a roof and a meal, and this his wife. As if to prove it to me, he said to her at once:

"We've a guest, Rosemay, a minstrel, no less. Fetch us ale, my lass, and hurry the food."

And she, to help the proof, Heaven forgive her, said to him in a voice lilting and pure as my harp itself: "Yes, husband."

She said it with liking, too. With love, even, though that she should love him was beyond me. Me she never glanced at.

Well, I'm young. Flat-bellied, long-legged, strong and

limber. I've good teeth, and women like my hair and my face, or so they tell me, and the rest, too, should we come to such dealings. My voice, I know, is better than most. So I spoke to her, I did, to the old sheepman's tawny Rose.

"Thanks for your generosity, lady."

But, "Be at ease," said she, and still she did not glance. Not even at the 'lady' I'd gifted her, shepherd's wife that she was. Then she brought the ale in a skin, and two wooden cups. She poured his, firstly. The fire flared, showing me, as of a purpose, her young smooth skin. She was not more than sixteen, and he a world-bitten forty. Men will often die before they are forty in the South, but here they live longer. There's a strange still power in this land. The hills hold it, and men can take it to them if they will. So I've heard, and so I believe.

Well, next she came to pour for me, and as she put the cup in my hand, our fingers brushed, and as she leaned to fill the cup, the slope of her breast pressed against the bodice of her gown. And more than one cup was filled. I lusted for her, but it was more than that. The sight of her in the doorway, her voice, her sheen, her eyes – which now I saw were not blue, or brown, but the shade of that stone they mine for hereabouts, partly black and partly amber – all this thrilled me, devilled me. I had the feeling, more than to lie with her, to lift her up, to make her into music, like a new, bright bird-winged song.

As soon as she was finished pouring ale, she went over to the cooking place and never once had she looked at me.

So it went on, then. We had supper, a tasty mutton stew and slabs of bread with the crust yet warm on them. She waited on us, not sitting to her own food till we were served, and she serving him always the first, smiling at him once, when he raised his shaggy brows, and never noticing me. I fancy, if another maid had been so circumspect, I might have guessed her shy or sly and begun to hope. But this one's way was not like that, but rather as if I were invisible – like that absent guest they will lay a place for at the table and serve with food, though neither he nor anyone sits there. During the meal there was no conversation, for this was no castle board; one thing came at a time. When we had had our fill – I asking an extra portion, a thing I rarely do in a poor house, but to get her attention, and not getting it – she took the bowls out to cleanse them. The shepherd meanwhile fished a hunk of meat from the stew, and moved just outside the door with it, whistling his dog. I'd thought it odd not to have seen a dog before, and odder yet when, through the doorway, I saw one come skulking down the hillside by the sheep, as if it had done something bad. I followed the man, and stood leaning on the doorpost. The gloaming was fading at last, but I could see Rosemay, walking over the turf with the bowls. The dog, as it sidled towards the cot, slunk by her and ran to the man, snatched the meat from his grasp, and made off at once, back up the hill with it. The shepherd turned, and with a grunt went by me into his house. I, amused a little at the dog, which treated the woman somewhat as she had treated me, strolled forward in the gloom to intercept her.

"The dog does not like you, it's plain. Silly, witless dog."

"It is my husband's dog," was all she would say, and was gone by me again, into the house to her elderly mate.

I went in after them with a silent oath, leaving the great landscape of Dark Hills to wind itself away on the spindle of night. Now I'd play for them, for a bargain is a bargain.

I'd play, and see what that would do. I have had women weep, even swoon at my songs, or they pretended they did.

He, when I took up my harp and let it from its cover, gave off that slight unfathomable noise the audience, large or small, will generally give, settling itself. Naturally, I squinted, too, over my tuning, to see how she did. But she sat motionless beyond the fire, though she had taken up no piece of women's work to mask her idleness. It seemed she would listen. Well, then.

I sang some songs, I forget now which they were, the usual sort with which one begins, catching the mood, or making it. The shepherd relaxed, smiling and nodding, sometimes drumming his fingers in time. But my tawny rose, she sat as if a bee were buzzing in the room. So I came to the song I wanted. It was an old romance, old as the Dark Hills themselves, maybe, and it travels under many names and manier guises. But the gist of it is this: A young minstrel-knight falls deep in love with the woman of his liege lord, so deep in love he forgets battle and loyalty and honour for her sake, though he tells her nothing of the affair. And this I sang, and when I came to the tally of the woman's virtues, I made them hers, her hair, and parti-colour eyes, her honey skin. Even the royal lady's gown was saffron, in my song. It was a fly thing to be doing, you'll say, but I reckoned him too unparticular to rouse at it. He seemed half asleep as it was. And she. What would she do?

She sat with her chin on her hand, and her eyes downcast, but she was very still now, so still I could not see her breathe, and in the shadow beyond the fire, she seemed scarcely to be there.

Then I struck the chords, and told how the minstrel-knight, who loved so unrequitedly and so well, resolved to redeem his honour, and died in the war of his master, died with twenty-seven wounds in his young body, and not one of these at his back. And when he lay with his fair noble face lit by the sky, the very clouds wept for pity. And his men took him to the castle, and the royal woman grew pale when she was told, and went to visit his corpse. As she bent over him, one single tear she could not restrain fell on his lips, at which they parted and his soul spoke to her from within the cadaver: *Lady, this is not death to me, for I died long ago when first I looked on you. I ask your prayers who never did ask your love.*

I sang dulcetly. I had something at stake. The song, which is a worthy one, and not easy to play, came sweetly, and moved me. It is a tale warranted to overthrow a maid, but I admit there were tears in my own eyes, when I looked for hers.

But she did not sit crying. For a moment I believed I had cast my glove at the moon, as they say, and wasted the effort.

And then her gaze came up like two jewels in the shadow.

She stared full at me, and such a stare it was I felt burned to my very marrow, as if I had been shot with fire. And I own I trembled, too. For these eyes said, sharp and plain as swords: Oh, *I* would give you more than tears.

The shepherd was slumped, aware in a daze the music was over. As he bestirred himself, she got to her feet, his Rosemay, and without a word she drifted to the ladder like a blowing leaf, and up it she went. And he, the big dull ram, shambled after her, grumbling some phrase of approbation at me I was too fey, by now, to understand. On the mid-rung of the ladder, however, he bent on me a weird grin that did alarm me for an instant, as if he knew it all, and other things that I did not. But then he was gone, and I took it for imagining.

Alone, I sat, and I vow I waited.

The dusk was gone, night come, and the peats on the fire slumbered and went out. The very night slumbered, and those broad shoulders of land outside the door, if ever they do sleep, were sleeping too. For him, I heard him snore after a while. Then my pulse ran, to be sure. I sat, and I waited, in the fireless dark, to hear the soft sole of her foot on the rungs of the ladder, whispering like grass, or the rustle her hair might make.

Once, some tiny night-beast, having got in under the door or by the chimney, flew against my cheek, and the blood tumbled in me, for I mistook it for her fingers.

Then I lapsed somewhat, and lay down; I was tired enough for that, though not to sleep, I thought, in my fever. A man, having seen her eyes in that one gaze, could not have slept.

Strung tense as a bow-string I reclined there. Presently the moon rose, and slid in at the cracks in the door and between the stones of the wall, and finally through the chimney hole overhead. Then I told how late it had got, and that she had not come to me. Well, she might linger to be sure of him. Next, the moon went down. Supposing she was virtuous? But what had this to do with virtue? I had wooed her – wooed, mark, not – thieved – wooed and won her. This night she was rightfully mine.

Yet the night would soon be done.

I dozed, and I dreamed she stepped from the ladder and leaned over me and kissed my forehead, but I woke and it was the morning breeze fluttering from the chimney. The shaft of light was nearly blue, and when I opened the door to look out, the sky was like a plate of silver behind the black foldings of the hills. It had a comely scent, the morning, but stale and vile to me. It seemed she had dallied with me, made a mock of me after all. She cleaved to her old shepherd, and would have none of me, be I young as day and strong and handsome as a hero. So. Her loss, not mine.

I walked from the cot, my harp on my shoulders, sour and heavy, cursing both of them, and under all strangely puzzled, strangely ill-at-ease. For nightlong I had heard him shift about above, but never a sound from her. And when I glanced back from the brow of the ridge beyond the cot, I saw the whiteness of the may tree, and I remembered the well and how I had not come on her there; and later I remembered, too, how the dog had avoided her. A witch, perhaps, was golden Rosemay, and I ensorcelled one whole night, writhing, with her flame on me she had not deigned to quench.

Now you may suppose that is all my tale, and be wondering why I puffed it up as such a curiosity, and laugh at me, reckoning I was only astonished, being vainglorious, that a woman said 'no' to me. But indeed, there's something more to be told. If you'll be patient, you shall have it.

Three mornings after I walked from the cot, I reached a village under the hills. It was of stone, as they are in these parts, a prospering place, and busy, for it was market day. No harper in his right wits will pass a market by, and accordingly I chose my spot and conjured my songs and collected some coin – when they could hear me for the bleating of their goats. At noon, I paused for ale, and as I was drinking it, I heard one man say to another: "Mad Rose is about again."

That name, of course, stayed me. I turned my head, and a second man spoke up.

"Aye, and there's the harper listening."

"Who is mad, then?" said I.

"I'll tell you," said the gossip, "for it'd likely make a fine song." At that, I must buy him ale, which I did. Sometimes, in this way, you do get a yarn worth refashioning with music. He supped his drink a minute, then he began. "It's simply told. One market day a young man drove five of his sheep to our village, and on the street he met with our Rose. Now Rose was beautiful, and her hair was done up with ribbon, and she in her yellow dress, for you know how a maid is at market. But Rose was worse than most. A minx, Rose was, spoiling for every man, looking at him with her eyes till he thought he might do as he pleased, and then she'd run off, or set him at some other man's throat. There was near-murder done now and then, and Rose at the edge of it.

"She had no father, do you see, only a sickly mother could not keep rein on her. Then the young shepherd drove in his five ewes, and he saw Rose, and she danced for him like the rest, first not looking at him, as if he were invisible, and then darting a stare at him fit to have him catch alight. Now he was an honest lad, this shepherd. Before the evening came on, he went to the mother and offered to have Rose wed him. The mother, be sure, would have been glad to give her daughter away, but Rose, why she laughed and she made sport of him, and when he only stood in her mother's house, hanging his head for shame, Rose took up a pitcher of slops and emptied them over his crown. Now when she did that, his mildness left him, and they say he bellowed like a bull with rage. While outside, his sheep dog, that had lain quietly by the door, began to bark and howl as if it had the madness."

The gossip hesitated, his ale drunk down, to see if I would replenish it. But my heart was striking me in the side. I made no move and, good-natured enough, he went on.

"Well then, they say that he said this to our Rose: 'I will have you, whether you will or not. And you will be true to me and obedient to me, and fetch the water, and cook my food and pour my ale, and lie by me in my bed all night. And that bold barren look you flaunt shall be only for those others I let see it, and you will be hid from those I wish not to behold you. But on me you'll smile and fawn and be always with me, and that I swear.' And this said, he called the snarling dog, and they went off along the hills, leaving Rose cawing with mirth like a crow."

The man looked at his ale-pot again, less a reminder now than a perusal, feeling for the next words, for he was good at his story-telling, was the gossip.

"Now who knows but that the shepherd might have returned and carried her off, but he did not. There was fever about that spring, he took it, and he died, and the dog lay down on his feet and died too, and was buried with him under the may tree by the well, for the priest would not put this shepherd in the safe earth beside the church. The priest pronounced him a waerlog, and there may be something in that. For I've met those say they've spoken with a shepherd at dusk, near that well, and he grizzled by his forty-first summer, which he would have been, had he lived. As for Rose, she went lunatic on the night he died. Mad as the moon, and no help for it. They keep her indoors when they can, but sometimes she'll get loose and mope about. A sight it's a pity to see. But the notion is she's no more mad than you or I, but has only lost her soul. For the shepherd took it, and keeps it by him to do all he said, in her exact likeness as she was that day, sixteen and a rose, when he first set eyes on her."

I peered at him as if I too were crazed. I shook from head to heel. And then the other man touched my wrist and pointed behind me, and a silence fell on the inn.

I turned, what else? And turning I saw her, as before, coming in at a doorway. And yet not as before. Mad Rose.

Truly, she was a pitiful sight as he'd said, her elf-locks wizened to grey, yet still weeded by a girl's yellow ribbon, her maid's yellow gown, once moulded on a slender ripeness, now slack, raddled and grimed by more than twenty years' soiling.

She was forty, and a hag; old as the earth she looked, her

brown skin loose on her bones as the gown was loose on the frame of her. Her eyes were filmed and colourless and darted all about, but here and there they fixed on a man with a fierce and intimate stare,

I went chill to my blood. I was faint, and put my head down on the table, so I did not see them coax her away, though dimly I heard her screaming. Nor did she go quite away, for she stays in my mind, in either shape, eldritch or maiden, mad woman or rose soul.

I told you, the Dark Hills are enduring, and men can draw power from them. When once I leave, I shall not come here again.

A Night on the Hill

At the end of the yellow afternoon, Hone walked out of the waste and saw the village lying before him on the slope under the hill. The hill he had seen for some miles, he had made it his landmark. It looked softer and greener than the rocks of the desert he had been travelling for three days, and this was so. It was a verdant hill, covered by woods, and underneath the village basked on the bank of a little river, painted houses and vineyards, and goats in the meadow.

Hone was a big man, tall, brawny and fat, and though there was no hair on his head and he had no eyebrows or lashes, a beard sprouted from his face and hung to his belly, full of things he never bothered to comb away. He wore a bandit's case of leather and brass; in his belt were three knives of varying and exaggerated size. Now Hone grinned, and his six remaining front teeth put the watchers on the village street in mind of a happy hungry jackal.

"Hey you!" shouted Hone. "Fetch your headman!"

And when response was not immediate, he strode up to the nearest villager and belted him senseless with his brass-knuckled fist. The others of course ran to do Hone's bidding.

Hone looked round. He was thinking over to himself all the good things that were obviously on offer here. He had found villages like this in the past, and he always enjoyed a long and prosperous stay. Some even had treasures in gold and jewels tucked away, in their temple perhaps, (Hone was neither religious nor superstitious.)

Back came the mobile villagers with their headman, who had a small ruby in one ear.

"You'll give me that," stated Hone, pointing.

The headman, already sweating and swallowing, inquired why he should.

Hone, instead of knocking him over, encircled the headman's shoulders with one meaty arm. In a friendly tone, he set about enlightening him. "You see, dearie, if you and yours don't do exactly as I say, my mates, who are a few days behind me on the road here, will make a nasty mess of you all when they arrive. That's if *I* don't make a nasty mess first. And Hone tweaked the headman's nose playfully, causing it to bleed. "Got a daughter?" he added.

"Two," choked the headman. He appended carefully, "Sir."

Hone asked their ages, plumpness, and at the reply his grin broadened.

The surviving villager said, "This gentleman and his mates have obviously come here because of the hill."

Hone reckoned he was quick, and life had never lessoned him otherwise. Now he turned, and in the westering rays of the sun, squinted at the wooded slopes above the village. He noticed that none of the goats grazed there, though the grass was lush, and that no part of the hill had been cleared to make a field or vineyard. There were no tracks. The houses stopped in a row at the hill's foot. But for now he only said, "What's for dinner?" And urged them to lead him somewhere for a feast.

Hone dined lavishly in the headman's hall, waited on by the headman's shivering wife and sister, who, being too mature for Hone's taste, he merely tormented, spooning scalding soup on their wrists and wiping off butter in their hair. Since he had demanded each of the important men of the village be present, there they were, and by calling on the headman's wine casks, Hone had seen to it that all were fairly drunk.

As the sun began to sink through the fine glass window, Hone addressed the frightened and addled company.

"*Now* tell me about this hill of yours."

A silence resulted. Hone freed a knife and turning to one of his neighbours, the baker, he cut off one of his fingers. "What did I say?" asked Hone.

"The hill is enchanted."

"Demons and weird spirits have charge of it."
"No one dares venture there."
"Who would want to?" said Hone, craftily.
"Many have wanted to. Legend says there's treasure at the top of marvellous value," said the village scribe. "They go by night –"
"Why fear the hill?" interrupted Hone.
"Whoever goes up there," said the village blacksmith in a loud voice, "is never seen or heard of again. Two men went up the hill one night in my boyhood. One was betrothed to my sister, who he loved, and the other too had good reasons to come back. But neither man was ever seen after that night."

Hone brooded in thought. Though to help his cogitations, he reached over to his other neighbours, the butcher and the carpenter, and cracked their heads together.

Undoubtedly something valuable was on the hill, for often these tales of banes and vanishments surrounded such hoards – in order to keep off fools.

Presently Hone spoke. "It's my bedtime, where's the bed?" And he threw a heel of bacon at the headman's wife.

Naturally, Hone did not entirely trust the villagers. Therefore he did not call for the plump daughters, but lay on the headman's bed – now his own – until the village was in darkness. Then Hone got up, sidled out, and took his way off up the hill.

The moon was high, and white as if afraid. The stars shone like knife points. It was black under the trees, but shadows did not trouble Hone. There was nothing else there, certainly, and in the scared-clear moonlight Hone did not discern the trails of foxes; he disturbed no feeding hare, heard no sound but his own footfalls and the slosh of the wine he had brought.

But there was nothing in that. The climb was long but not difficult, for Hone was strong and used to exercise.

He reached the hill's summit as the moon was going down the other side.

Up on the hill top was a ring of perfect quiet so intense Hone might have been dropped in there like a pebble, but the ripples he made were silence. The hill top was, in addition, bare of anything. Hone stamped about, not pleased, until his foot kicked against a square flat stone set into the ground. The bandit knelt, and putting his largest knife under this stone, levered it up. On show then, in the departing moonlight, was an empty hollow in the earth. Cursing, Hone peered into it. There were only some pale shards of stone lying in the hollow. Hone realised they spelled the words *gone away*.

Hone jumped to his feet, knife much in evidence. A trick? He glared snarling at the trees, but no one was there. Only silence sat on the hill with Hone wriggling in her lap.

Presently, very much discouraged, the bandit sat also, and fell asleep with his back to the tree, dreaming vengeance on the village in the morning.

And while he slept, an owl circled the hill once, but did not fly over it.

Up with the lark was Hone the next day.

The sun rose to meet him as he hurtled down the hill in great bounds, making chopping motions with his knife in the air.

He gained the village by midmorning, and was delighted to see the main street full of men and women and several plump maidens, most of whom were looking towards the hill with strange wild faces.

"Here I come!" yelled Hone, leaping off the last slope, and bursting out before the crowd. "You rabbits' phlegm, now you'll learn what it is to make a joke at Hone's expense!"

The crowd stared on, transfixed.

Hone came to the bandaged baker, and shouted in his face: "You're first!" And something odd struck Hone. The baker did not flinch or try to draw away. The baker only stared, unmoved, straight through Hone and up the hill.

Hone lashed out with his knife. He meant to take off the

baker's nose, and was astonished when he missed. He tried again. The baker's nose stayed pristine before him. So then Hone bashed the baker in the face – and Hone saw his own arm had passed right through the baker and out the other side, and when he drew it back again, it left the baker standing there unblemished and – worse – in complete ignorance of the blow.

"Here I am," said Hone to the baker cautiously.

Then to the village, and the world, he bellowed: "Here! *Here!*" But no one looked at Hone, no one listened. And those he touched and pushed and thumped and finally pulled at and begged, these did not see him or hear him, or feel him either. His hands and knives went through them like smokes, and through everything indeed.

"Well," snuffled the headman to the crowd, "this time it was lucky for us, the hill."

"Whoever goes there goes by night," said the scribe.

"And is never more seen or heard of," smugly finished the headman's wife.

And it is a fact, Hone never was seen or heard of, ever again.

Seeing, Believing

(From an Idea by Mike Ashley)

You say my English is quite good now. So I will write this for you in English. You won't believe it. What an imaginative story, you'll say. And give me a little prize. I should like the metric ruler, please, with the golden tiger painted on both sides.

When I was in my village, one day Ranjish said to me, "What is it like, Meera, not being able to see?"

And I said, "I don't know." But then I thought, and I said, "You say when the elephants come to drink at the river, they have long noses that are *trunks*."

"Yes," said Ranjish, "so they do."

"Well," I said, "suppose one of the elephants said to you, what is it like, Ranjish, not having a trunk?"

Ranjish laughed. "I don't know, Mrs Elephant."

"It's like that for me," I said. "I don't know what it's like, not having something I never had."

I was born blind, and my mother and sisters cried for days. I think one of the old women said I shouldn't have been born at all. But my father said, "This is her life, this time. And she must live it."

In my world there was everything. All these sounds and smells, and touching things, and the warmth of them, and the coolness. I remember all those pulses of heat and cool and wet and stillness and *movement*. And the noises of them all. The daytime house was spice and sweat and smoke, and the grain I learned to grind for bread, and the sticky smell of the rice. My sisters singing, and me singing, and the radio with its nice songs playing. And at night, the smell changed. After-scents of food, and clean skin from washing, and spilled water, and my father's cigarettes.

Outside – goats, smooth, prickly, butting, going *"maaa"*.

Strong goat smell, loud with health. And perfumes that now I think have colours all their own, from the women's hair and clothes. And milk, the village smells of milk. And powdered earth. And beyond the village is the forest.

The forest has other smells and other sounds. In parts of the year the forest smells wet, and at different times like dry fire. Monkeys scream, and their shadows go over in a flash of cool. Frogs go like clocks – tick, tick, click, clock. Parrots – like funny musical instruments. Smell of feathers. Smell of sun on feathers and leaves, and deep wet places.

The old women, some, said, "She will go where she shouldn't, the blind one. Tread on a snake. Meet tiger."

My father, who told me stories, said to me, "Snakes sound like this." And he pulled something – was it his tie for the town? – through the dust, and then through the leaves in the scented bush by the door. "Tiger is hot," said my father.

My mother said, "If you know the tiger comes, kneel down, as you do to the gods. Bow your head and speak softly. *Praise* him. He'll let you alone."

Our gods live in the house by one wall. But really, they're over the sky, and everywhere. They smell sweet from the honey and butter and milk offerings, and from the little flame that burns there. They feel smooth as the smoothest stone. Something comes from them, too. Not smell or touch.

A *feeling*. You can be afraid of it, or just not worry, just give in. And then it's kind. Kind like a father or mother.

Kind like *very soft*.

Last year when I was, you told me, ten, I walked down the village street. And the old women loudly whispered "Look at her, the blind one. Look at her blue eyes." Which I thought just meant my eyes looked nasty to them. But the old women sounded nasty to *me*.

By the well, where the smell of the wet is, cold, warm, and I could hear the grasshoppers singing, Ranjish came up, with the sense of Ranjish, Coca-Cola and bounce and running about. "Come to the ruined temple, Meera."

"I want to get some water."
"Get the water, then come."
"All right."

But Ranjish got the water, hauling it up, and I only took the pot. He shouldn't have done that. It seemed he liked me. What does he look like?

We haven't got a word for 'Thank you', or for 'Please'.

I expect you know this. It's because no one is supposed to have to plead for anything, and if anything is given them, then it should be given freely. So, no please, no thank you.

After the water, I came back. I said to Ranjish, "Which temple?" I hope you notice I say in English *'Which'*. That's correct grammar, isn't it? I do want that ruler, for the tiger.

Of course, I'm translating what I really said. What I really said wasn't like that. Ranjish said that some trees had been cleared a bit, and a temple had appeared out of the depths of the forest, all covered in creepers. But the temple was haunted by a demon, or ghost.

"Who says so?"

Then the others, who had come up, laughed. "Everyone says so. The man who drives the bus – the old man who wanders about – Mrs Heaven, (that is the proper translation of her name), who went there after a stray cow – she said a ghost came out and she felt it was near and ran away in terror."

"What is it like?"

Ranjish said, "No one has *seen* it."

I don't know if Ranjish knew, when he said that, how I'd feel. Maybe not.

But I thought: No one *sees* the ghost. I don't *see* anything. Here's something they can't do like I can't do. (Or is it, *as* I can't do...?)

So, I went.

Which wasn't good, because I had things to help with in the house, with my mother, who has six other daughters, and I am the seventh.

The old women whispered behind me, like the

grasshoppers. I think they turn into grasshoppers, in the end.

In the forest, one of the girls tried to guide me, but Ranjish explained she didn't need to. I sensed things – could *feel* them, a sort of different air around them. So I didn't bang into trees, or step on sharp stones, or fall.

Ranjish seemed proud of me. This was nice. But then we came to the temple.

How to tell you about this? I know, you would *look*, and see, how walls went up, and the pavilions of old marble, and lattice screens with lots of little holes the sun shone through. And great creepers, and flowers, and birds flying away.

Well, I could smell the marble – wet-dry smell. And smell the cool of the shadow falling between us and the sun. And the key-holes of light. And hear the clatter of wings. The temple was *heavy*. I could feel it hanging there. Sky open and then turned into stones.

We went in.

I heard them whispering, not like the old women. And then I knew they'd gone, Ranjish and the other boys, and the girls. I felt their warmth and spice-smell and live-skin smell melt away.

They had brought me, then left me.

In the past, sometimes people had been cruel to me. I mean, like when the little girl who was my cousin tried to make me put my hand in the fire I couldn't see. But of course I felt the fire before I touched it. And other things.

Now they'd brought me here into the temple and left me, for the demon-ghost.

I turned around. It was cold, and – dark. Yes, it must have been dark. It felt the way I know dark is now. And heavy wet air.

Carvings – I felt them under my fingers. And water, cool, round water in a tank.

I sat on the edge of the tank. I thought, my father would come home, and he would know they'd brought me here.

Somehow he would. And he'd find me. I only had to wait.

And the gods knew as well. They see all things. There's no need ever to be afraid.

Then, the dark grew deeper, wetter, heavier.

And then – I saw the ghost.

I *saw* it.

This is hard to describe to you. You see, where you have eyes, where you *see* – for me, never. There was nothing. Just – *nothing*. Not darkness, or brightness. Just – an open closed space with not a thing in it.

But now, suddenly, there in that space, which normally for you, would have all sorts of images and colours, there was this – *thing*.

It was – I think now, I *think* it was – *blue*. Very pale blue, and very glowing. Inside my *head*.

I jumped up. I screamed. I heard my scream rush round the upper places of the temple, and bats rose like a wind. I could smell them.

But in my head, this thing – like a flame – stood, trembled, *was*. No smell, no sound. No *feel*. But I *saw* it. Saw – saw –

I was lying on the ground, but it came closer, it came and trembled over me. And then I saw the shape, and it was a shape, of course, I didn't understand. It was this way: (have I got the mark right? A dot over a dot – what do you call it? Colon:) A mass at the top, flowing and shifting. And then a long shape that went in a bit about halfway down, and under this split into two. But it split above that also, into two. And the two long upper parts waved about.

Then everything slowed down. And then it drew away. And it moved, still. But now, it moved in a sort of music. I mean, it was a pattern. It surged and shifted. The long upper split parts, and the upper mass, all lifting and flowing and the two lower split parts, all flowing. It was graceful. It was beautiful. And then I felt the beauty of it. After all, it had a feeling.

I sat up. I watched it. I remembered something from a story my father had told me. Then I realised that the ghost was dancing. And then I realised that what I had seen was a head with long hair, and two arms, and a body, and two legs.

I was like this too. This shape. Just the same.

Then the glowing ghost got smaller and smaller, and I knew it was going away.

I said, "Don't go." And then, "What shall I bring you?"

But the ghost got so small, and then it darted to one side, and vanished. I thought it had gone behind something. Something had hidden it from me, in the way it happens if you can see.

For a long while I stayed there, but the day was changing, growing late, so then I found my way down carefully, and as I was coming out into the warmer, thicker place that was the forest, I heard my father running up, calling me.

"Ranjish has been beaten," said my father, as he carried me home on his shoulders. I had forgotten Ranjish. "But someone has come to talk to you, my Meera."

I was sleepy. When we got home, my mother gave me a cup of milk, and then a man who smelled of disinfectant talked to me, as my father had said. It was the English doctor. He examined my eyes, gently, and his breath bloomed with mint.

Although he talked, I didn't understand most of what he said. None of us did, but for my father.

The doctor chewed gum; that was the mint smell. He left some for us all. It was good, but after you chewed for a while, it was only like chewing old bread that wouldn't ever go soft.

In the night, in the deep shadow-feel of night, my sister, the sixth daughter, who is only two years older than me, said, "In the temple – was there anything there?"

"Yes," I said.

"Liar," said my sister. "Just because the doctor came from the city. They always put you first. Little show-off." (She didn't say that, but that was what it meant.) And she hit me, under the covering. "*Was* there anything? Eh, Meera?"

"No," I said. "No."

I could hear my mother crying softly. When my sister slept, my father said to my mother, "The doctor says there is a good chance. But we have to wait."

Once or twice in the past, doctors had examined my eyes. What were eyes, anyway? You see, then, eyes didn't mean much to me.

That night I did something bad. I got up, and went out, and through the village, and into the forest. Our word for the forest isn't like *forest*. It means something more wild, greater, full of winds and beasts and huge trees. And secrets.

I wasn't afraid. You see, I had a dream, and in the dream, I saw the glowing thing, moving in its pattern.

I *saw* it.

Well, if you were an elephant and had never had a trunk; but one day, just for a minute, in a certain place, you *had* a trunk –

I went back through the forest and found the temple by its smell and the feel of its stone, and the sense of its heaviness.

Inside, I climbed up. The bats were awake too, and the creeper seemed to be. I knew the way now to the tank of water. I stood there and felt the starlight through the cleared trees, and starlight *feels* just how it looks. I suppose, everything does.

After a while, she came.

Yes, it was a *she*. I knew, for she was like me. She was small, and she was wrapped in clothes, and even so, her legs could be glimpsed, moving, and her pattern that was a dance. Her hair shook out, and bracelets jangled on her wrists, but I couldn't hear them. I could *see* them.

I said, "I came back, lady." I wanted to be polite. "I didn't bring you anything, I didn't know if you'd like anything – except this packet of mint chewing gum. I'll leave it here."

But she only danced. She didn't seem to care about the gum.

She danced, she must have done, for hours. And I sat in the chilly night on the cold marble, and *watched*. I *watched*. The blind one, seeing.

And then, probably, the morning started, for a warmth came that would be a colour, and birds called.

And then she danced towards me, and I stood up.

I know when you read this, you'll say, Meera, it's a ghost story. But it isn't *frightening*. Silly Meera!

But it wasn't. Not frightening. Even though she came so close, the glow of her filled all my – all my *sight*. So it was just one glowing blue flame in my head. Except I didn't know then, the look of flames or blue.

She made no sound. There was no scent or touch.

But she must have passed right over me, or through me. Because after that she was gone.

I got up stiff and cold, and walked back through the forest, and in the village I pretended I had only gone to pick the flowers by the roadside that my mother likes and that I had smelled growing there.

When I gave her the flowers, she burst out crying.

"Oh Meera, my baby. My poor little Meera."

My oldest sister is to be married soon. Only *she* wasn't jealous.

After my mother let me go, they came, one by one and pinched me, and one pulled my hair.

I felt so sleepy, and there was no time now to sleep. I knew I mustn't go back to the temple.

When I was fetching water, Ranjish threw a stone at me, because he had been beaten.

That evening, to everyone's surprise, the doctor came back. He said he would drive my mother and me straight to the station in the town next day. Then we would all go to the city, and they would change my eyes.

"There's every chance," he said. He kept saying that. He had brought sweets and coffee. Everyone got happy.

Except me. I was scared.

Outside, I could hear the old women whispering about knives.

Seeing, Believing

The train was hot and horrible. It lasted a day. We got out sometimes to refresh ourselves. You would say, to use the toilet, which was a bush. There was some nice orange drink, very sweet.

My mother held me. She would hardly let go.

In the hospital it was cool and fans like great buzzing flies blew round and round.

Everyone was kind. They made me go to sleep. When I woke up I was sore, my *eyes* were sore, I could *feel* them. I was covered in bandages and yet, something was quite different.

I won't describe it all, because I'm not writing about that. *You* came to visit me after the bandages were off and everything had changed.

At first, only shapes, and then the shapes were clear. So *this* is a hand. And *this* is a foot. And there was so much movement and light and – *colour*. I know I would have been frightened more than I could bear, at first, if I hadn't ever seen before. But I had. I'd seen – her.

I didn't tell you about her. You brought me the furry cat toy, pale like you and dark like me. I liked him. You told me about this school. You said, in English, I was "Bright". What a strange word. *Bright*. Like a fire. Or the moon. Or your dress.

I knew, when I went home, they would sit and look at me, all my sisters, and hate me, in a row. Except the oldest, who is going to be married. And she'd say, "Look, Meera can be married now." But my father would say proudly, "Meera is at school and will be a doctor." My mother would clasp her hands. Which will be worth a lot of pinching.

But my father said Ranjish has gone away with his uncle. My father wore his tie, when he said it. It is red.

When I saw myself in a mirror, I laughed. There I was. How wonderful I was, like everyone and everything else.

When I go home, I don't want to go back to the temple, because I know I won't see anything *there* at all. I only saw her because I was blind.

That's why I want the ruler, you see. Because I never saw a

tiger, and there aren't many tigers now, in the forest. And so I'd like to look at the tiger on the ruler. Probably I'll never see another one.

But only give me the ruler if you think I deserve it. And if you don't believe my story, I don't mind. Because I know it's true. As true as the forest and the train and the city and seeing and my cat.

Meera.

Meera. I've given you a high mark, and you shall have the ruler. Now I want to tell you a story, too.

The temple in the jungle by your village was visited long ago, a hundred years or more, before the trees hid it.

It is said to be haunted, by a dancing girl. I read this in the library this afternoon, and I'll show you the book. It's in English, but your English is so good, you can easily read it.

The dancing girl haunts the temple because she was so happy there. She died when she was ten – one year younger than you are now. We believe, don't we, she will have gone to another place, and been born again as someone else. So this isn't really a *ghost* – more a *very* happy *memory*.

You see, Meera, she was born blind, but her dancing was wonderful, and it pleased the gods. People still hear her laughing sometimes, in the temple, or the sound of her bracelets, or they smell her perfume, or feel her brush by.

No one has ever seen her – *but you.*

The Sky Won't Listen

"...by the blending cadence of waves with thoughts... at last he loses his identity; takes the mystic ocean at his feet for the visible image of that deep, blue, bottomless soul, pervading mankind and nature; and every strange, half-seen, gliding, beautiful thing that eludes him; every dimly-discovered, uprising fin of some indiscernible form, seems to him the embodiment of those elusive thoughts that only people the soul by continually flitting through it. In this enchanted mood, thy spirit ebbs away to whence it came; becomes diffused through time and space... forming at last a part of every shore the round globe over."

—Herman Melville
Moby-Dick

"He prayeth best, who loveth best."
—Samuel Taylor Coleridge
The Rime of the Ancient Mariner

1. Grey in High Egypt

My name's Maud Ruby.

I'm old now, but when young my long hair was red, quite a showy red too. *Ruby* comes from this, while *Maud* goes back to an ancestor of mine on Oldearth.

She wouldn't know me, I doubt she would, out here among the New Planets. Come to that, I don't really know myself. They tell you that you'll get to know yourself better as you age up. But I knew myself better when I was twenty-five, or forty –

that redhead who drank white wine and worked at Stargaze. This other one I live in now, who's she?

I was sitting in a casbar called *The Silk Market* and drinking more than wine, as now I do. The place was fetchingly decorated in black, silver, grey, pink and damson, to match the geography and skies of the planet. Most of the city of High Egypt is like that, and by day you could hardly make it out from the surrounding terrain. They seemed to tint the local fauna too. Pink pigeons roosted on 4th Walk, by the canal they call High Nile. The people favoured the same colours. Even I toned, dressed in my pale skin, by now chopped-at-the-shoulders grey hair, and black clothes. Not my liver, maybe. That will be gamboge, I guess.

While I drank I waited for a message from Apharis, but the little LT stayed blank. So I looked about at the other drinkers, and wondered if any of them had ever heard of Lir McCloud, the ballineer.

Then they were staring out one of the windows. So I stared out too.

There was a whale in the sky.

I hadn't seen any till then, and this was a large example, and passing over quite low. Earth-ocean whales are beautiful enough, once you can mentally cope with the idea of their sheer size. The sea Whalons of Titanus are even more impressive, if less aesthetically so. But the Ballin sky whales of New Planet Z/d7 are one of the wonders of worlds. Apparently similar in many ways to the earth type of spermaton, they're easily that size once described as *big as islands*. Covered with scars, aerial barnacles and other tropo-stratospheric funguses, from a reasonable distance they look wet-sleek as a satin evening-glove. In colour they range from plum or puce to thunder-black. They gleam and shimmer, moving with unforgivably incomparable grace, through the shoals of pollution junk-cloud, storm out-banks, and occasional wary off-course aircraft. When, as this one had, they sail down low, the flocks of pigeons and flits disperse in tea-leaf showers before them. The whales of Z/d7 don't feed on birds or planes. They suck and nibble nutrients from the cumulus and drink the unborn rain. They never fight that anyone knows, and they mate and birth up there. They only touch ground when they die, and for that they seek the open deserts. Unaggressive giants, they seem never to aim to do harm. And even fifty years ago they were only hunted by pioneers for the sake of their skins that, when treated after death, glow lamplike in the dark, or for the whale-ivory of their hollow bones, which make musical instruments of such sweet clarity.

Not a sound in the casbar but for the clink of glasses or rattle of auto-dice from the casino room. Then someone swore. "The soonest they move those fucking critters outta here the better. Ruining this bloody town."

No one either challenged or agreed. (From what I'd read or seen, opinion was evenly split).

Nevertheless the guy swung his thick neck around to see if anyone might.

I wasn't quick enough to duck. He tramped right over.

"Damn fuck whales oughta be shot down. Oh yeah yeah, I know IRS[1] are rounding up whale pods, relocating them – so what's holding everything up? Fancy word that, *relocate*. But to where? That's what I wanna know. Basinopolis? Clovial Peak? Huh?"

"Mmm," I said.

"And two-thirds of 'em to get relocated. How about three-thirds?'

Something moved in my mind. I'm so used to it by now. Not like my training days at Stargaze, when sometimes it wouldn't, then it might, or not. Now, reliable as breathing. Mindscape.

I saw the big boy's jaw slacken and his eyes go cloudy as hate drained from them. Quietly I said, "And how about you have a nice day?"

"Sure... sure –" He lurched off into the casino.

---

[1] IRS Indigenous Rescue Service

In the sky the beautiful colossus had drifted toward the horizon. A light unseasonal spat of hail scattered on High Egypt – whale weather. For they did harm after all, the whales.

They disturbed the cloud masses when they passed low, the ionosphere when they moved up, and all points of the atmos in between. A small, peripatetic pod doesn't matter, its effect is negligible. But the concentration of whale-kind gathering and loitering above the cities was by now intense – pods of one to two thousand, which en masse put out the light of the sun. Given time, Ballin wreck the local tropo-stratosphere. Then come freak storms, droughts, flood-rains, acid snows, sky-debris of several alien sorts. This had happened already at Basinopolis and Clovial.

Why the whales were attracted to centres of humanity no one figured. Men had never been their friends in the past. As I said, they were hunted through the skies, and in those days High Egypt was the prime whaler port.

I glanced at the LT; still no message.

I ordered another drink.

Wish I's in High Egypt
How happy I ud be —
Ev 'body know High Egypt you
Can pick the money offa tree —
All day long
The sun is strong
All through a night
The 'ol casbars is alight
An ' their music playing –
H'Egypt issa place for me.

I'd heard some of the old whaleship songs in the archive. Rendered in voices of gravel and smoke. Sad, silly, bawdy – and workmanlike to haul up a grav anchor by. Like all sailors on all ocean worlds, even in the vast ocean of space, they always wanted to be in some town when they were at sea, or at sea when they were home. Most of us are like this, one way and another. We want to be somewhere else. Even the future or back in the past. Some of us even hanker for the next life, if there is one. And if there is, when we get there maybe we crave to get back here.

Unlike men, the Ballin don't sing or make any communicative noise.

The message had come, and sunset was starting as I walked out to the docks. Magenta curtains closed the western mountains as far and further than Sphinx Ridge. But eastwards, north and True North (Z/d7 has two norths), the sky would stay icy white for another hour.

There were more whales passing, a pod-battalion this time, about two hundred. These animals swam higher. And along with others on the moving sidewalk, I gazed up. Nobody now made any comment.

One of the two moons rose, roughly east and barely visible.

Lights were coming on all around. After dark the camouflaged city showed up after all, outlined in the diamanté of fy-neon, like the song says. Two sides to everything.

They were tall, young and handsome people, the Indigenous Rescue Service crew of *Spanish Lady*.

The vessel herself was of the usual aerial small-craft type, modern and streamlined, an enclosed disc with just the central sail-vein mast projected upward to take prevailing winds. The old vessels that sailed such planet skies as these had been quite unlike. And though they would have recognised, probably, something like *Spanish Lady*, they wouldn't have liked her much. The whaleships were made to a more romantic programme, and besides not above disabling each other in order to get their cargo to port first.

Captains Apharis and Jenx led me straight to the Captains' Cabin, where we cracked a bottle of mauve sub-Lyran gin.

There wasn't much small talk. Their job was to carefully capture in air-nets and safely relocate whales to uncolonised areas of this big planet. But something had been preventing their work. And to deal with that would be the job which was mine.

I said, "So this is all about Lir McCloud."

I'd read the relevant records, of which there were few.

Apharis shrugged. "You've seen the damage hologs on our ships."

"Two vessels clipped, and one emergency landing. He *fired* on you?"

"Yes. But."

Jenx said, "He can't *fire* on us... can he?"

"Perhaps. What happened?"

They told me. The other ship had sprung from nowhere. Then the blast of fire – of course ineffectual – yet somehow two of the IRS craft were winged. The third one was tipped out of the sky.

"A form of Psy-kenesis," I said. "Luckily rare. It isn't physical, but can pack a punch."

They nodded, respectfully convinced.

Startling. Decades back I used to be well-known in my own small corners of the universe. But new talent rises. Here and there someone may yet exclaim to me, *Say, I read about you in this old book!* Astonished I am still alive and walking the worlds.

I informed the captains of what I'd be doing. By then *Spanish Lady*'s gravs had warmed to full power. I watched as we made lift-up through the ice sky and the fading purple, into a darkness where the city lost its glare, and instead the bright wasps of stars had left their silver-swollen stings.

What was hampering the rescue operation at High Egypt was a NAATH.[2] That is a recurrent, quasi-physical ghost. In form, it was a manned antique on-planet whaling vessel, the kind that had cruised these skies fifty to a hundred years before. Already the IRS, well read in Oldearth yarns, had christened her the *Flying Dutchman*. Her real name however, which all three menaced crews had noted, was *Perilune*.

---

[2] NAATH Non-Alive Apparency (having) Tactile Habitualness

Jenx, to look at, reminded me fleetingly of my second lover – I only ever had three true lovers in all my long years. Now, obviously, Jenx was much too young. At my age, (maybe I'm lucky), I can admire, but don't fancy young men. Conversely they present to me as those sons or nephews I never had or wanted, yet now can sometimes be momentarily fond of. What I am saying is, and at this point I feel bound to say it, I'd ceased ever to fall in love by the time I was sixty-two, and on Z/d7 I was seventy.

We were all on the bridge. Huge view ports made a half-ring, piercing the ship with ovals of shielded night. The solitary moon, white at last, made the upper atmos a miracle. The sheer *glamour* of the spatial skies leaves unmoved merely the blind or the fool. Seas are the same, surely. The physical worlds are the only way mankind can know the mystery of an unphysical God, until – or if.

Not a single Ballin was now to be seen.

"Empty air," said Apharis, very low. "That's usually been when –"

"What's that?"

"Ah," said Apharis. "Shit."

Every alarm on the bridge echoed her in shrill antiphony.

2. The Open Skies

She came out of a moonlit cloud. She hadn't been there, then she was. It was like looking at a holog made from an antiquarian photograph. Somewhere in my brain (the brain back-rooms, where the technicalities are evaluated and processed), I knew the two great masts full of sail were equipped with ethallic stras'ls, that it was the cranky grav engines gave off that choking chugging; that the elevation of the vessel's nose was her prow, complete with daggered sprit. But my mind, my eyes saw only the shining shell, the exact curves of the sailage. Certainly she was physical, sufficiently physical that she seemed entirely real and of that moment. She glowed in strangely neutral shades of colour – pastel sand, tired dust. Her name was scored on her side in an old-time font: *Perilune*. And the moon lit her to a pale pearl, like the ion clouds of the highest sky.

My mind was already pursuing its trained function. I'd noted men on her upper deck. The old ships, particularly whalers, weren't entirely closed. Rather like the ancient submarine of Oldearth, they *could* shut off their below-decks, if an ascent was made through or above the planet's ozone layer, but generally the top deck was in use.

Images. The crew of the ghost were shadows. Just there – or there – a flash of movement, glitter-flick of eyes or earring.

Even so, the entirely shut bridge of *Spanish Lady* reeked with the high-ozone discharge of an early grav-ship.

My inner mind slipped free of me. It uncoiled through the physical barriers of self and rescue ship. It ribboned like a whaler's harpoon-line across the gap, and fastened.

And so I found him. Lir McCloud.

His Oldearth ancestry (the archive) was Celtic, and he had retained the name, maybe amused at its new relevance. I couldn't, of course, see him as such. He was, like the rest, a shadow. But my mind – my mind *touched* him. My mind was trained and well-practiced in the art. Yet never before had it contacted anything, anyone, of this kind. It wasn't that he was dead, a remnant left hovering in limbo. I have contacted those. The oddity of this contact was – him. Or me. Me *with* him. Different. Like touching heat and cold, unalike, identical.

The NAATH ship had previously used her guns against IRS vessels. Being Psy-ken, the blow caused harm. *Lady's* shields were fully raised.

I had sensed inside his mind, that is, this afterimage of his mind that death had somehow marooned in the living world, the mental stain of the past. The flavour of Lir McCloud was restrained yet violent anger, bitter blame and self-denigration, despair.

He had registered, aged sixteen, as a freelance ballineer and novice harper, or harpooneer. Aged thirty-eight, and until then a successful captain, he had disappeared, and certainly died, along with his current ship, somewhere between outer-system space and the planet's F3 atmos layer. None of his crew were with him then. It seemed he'd driven them to mutiny by eccentric behaviour. But not one had left more testimony than that, and McCloud no testimony at all.

Now the ghost vessel floated there and the single moonlight dripped through her bones. Bit by bit, like wood in flame, she was eaten away, until she – and he, and all those shadows – were gone.

No one stopped me as I went to my cabin. Door closed, I used the auto to lock it and put out the lights.

Perilune might have fired, but she hadn't. She hadn't come for that. Her appearance was both a proof and an invitation. Not essentially to me, perhaps, but to someone. Now and then a mindscaper will encounter such a thing, and in my long career never before had I done so. And I'd been young then, physically fit, stronger, and, if less wise, also with less of the doubts all knowledge may bring.

Mindscape. I'd better put this down, in case someone reading this misunderstands the term; many do. To *mindscape* isn't essentially to recreate mentally or otherwise, (though that may be entailed), some view, or non-actual place. Entire, the term should read mind-*e*scape, mind-*escaper*. To get free of the fore-brain, even of the excellent encyclopaedic library and lab of the back-brain, and enter instead the physical astral plane of the inner gemynd, that awareness usually unfamiliar to and hidden from the consciousness – save for split seconds of memory or sudden rifts in dream – concealed even from the *sub*conscious, and utterly unknown to the id: the central domain, the open skies where we are as we *are*. Or, as we have always been, or will come to be, once dislocated from our *selves*.

Here's life to the living: long life to the skinners,
Keep um in cash and outa th'jail!
Keep um aloft and burny[3] their irons,
And strength in their backs while they follows the whale.

3. Ruby Red

There's a whale in the sky.

Just one, not so big, about sixty feet in length.

It's mulberry-purple, and casts a shade on the narrow byway outside the casbar, which isn't called *The Silk Market* but *The Whale's Eye*.

No one takes any notice tonight. They are used to whales, expect and *welcome* whales, one or two of which drift over every day or so. Sometimes you get a whole pod – fifteen to twenty creatures. The kids look up at the pods and afterwards play at slinging the stress-iron harpoons, (represented by thin sticks), and for hours not a dog or pigeon is safe in the mountain port of High Egypt.

Not a city yet, H'Egypt would laugh if you told it what it will become, and how decored. It doesn't try to match the sky. It is just paled dusts, dirty smoke and sand colours, like the houses, or human complexions. And the High Nile Canal is full of garbage.

Inside *The Whale's Eye*, however, a pair of beautiful tall fretted lamps goldenly beam day and night with whaleskin luminescence. To keep the light, all you need ever do is rub the skin fragments over every month or so with a little drop of plant oil. Living skin that, stripped from the corpse of a Ballin, never dies. Which accounts for one of the whaler nicknames, *skinners*. There is a giant, often played, pan-pipes hooked on the bar wall too, made from hollow Ballin bone. Skin and bones are

---

[3] Burny: Burnished, that is, polished *sharp*

what make the whales of Planet Z/d7 so well worth hunting.

Out at the docks, where the mountain-side crumbles down to Ship Valley, and the vaults of open air wait around and above, some thirty vessels are chained up this evening, prow-noses to land, and their stratos-sails (stras'ls) of ethallic metal closed tight as shut umbrellas to their masts. Ethallic is a mix of stress-steel, galvanized bio-copper and slyve P.9. Anchors of course are made of grain lead, containing cells of magnetic slyvium. Haul, haul her up, with the proper rhythm on the buttons, four anchormen: *Here's life to the living, long life to the skinners, keep um in cash...*

Maud is dressed in correct freewoman clothes of the town, where every street or alley is named for a sky ship or whaler captain, or some commodity of the whale. She wears long loose grey pants, tough boots for getting between the plank-built houses and over rocky tracks called maybe *Cap Chace Boulevard*, and not yet smoothed for sidewalks. Her shirt is clean, and she has two silver earrings, dollars that will be antiques in another thirty years. Her hair's red, henna red on fox red. She's aged twenty-five, because returning to the proper time via the navigation of the mindscape, she has retreated forty-five years into the past. This hasn't happened before. It is *his* past, when he was thirty-eight, and still alive. He's the ghost in her present-future. But now, she is the ghost inside the past of Lir McCloud.

Is it good to feel young and fit and fine again, Maud Ruby? To design an outfit to be seen in? Nice just abstemiously to sip your one schooner glass of cold white wine?

Piercing back like this into the astral-mind place, you always remember, *naturally* you do as you must, that this isn't you. It's projection. That you're young is – a boon. That's all.

But it's here, it's here and now, and you're in the midst of it, Maud the Escape Artist, sitting in the casbar called *Whale's Eye*, waiting for the captain of the *Perilune*, his fury, pain, his shadow, his secret self.

The door slams wide.

But it isn't McCloud, only some roisterers, who are going from joint to joint, playing card-games and diz-wheel, and getting drunk.

Maud gets up and goes out on the sidewalk. Not that Maud need fear any trouble, but there wouldn't be any from drunks – they treat women alone here with courtesy and respect.

Like the very whale colonies they hunt, the females are in charge 'at home,' caring for children, running the port.

The stars blaze over High Egypt, but the town isn't so well lit as it will be. At the docks the chained ships are lamped by skin, and rock gently on air currents. Maud walks by, and reads their names – *Lightgoal, Fin-Chaser, Be Home Tomorrow*. The clouds furl over the stars. Both moons are up, one against True North. (Although worlds move, they do so imperceptibly. Aside from animate, or animated things, only sky and water can be *seen* independently in volition. That is winds and clouds, rivers and tides and oceanic waves.) And other ship names – *Racing Girl, Perilune*.

"There you are," he says behind her.

Maud knows his voice. Though she's never previously heard it. It's lighter than she would have thought from his dark looks that she sensed, and now turns and sees. Oh, so this guy *knows* with fore-brain consciousness that they are to meet? That must be unusual.

"Here I am, Captain McCloud."

"Step aboard," he says.

But she doesn't have to. In the manner of an edited movie, or a dream, (which, when sleeping, involuntary mind-escapes can so often be taken for), she's suddenly on the ship, and already they are hauling the grav anchor in.

*Here's **life** –*

Stars cartwheel.

Seems five whale pods have been spotted, south and east. A couple of adjacent ships have lift-upped and taken off while she watched. No time to lose then, why let some other crew get all the skin. Anchor's up; in peels the chain.

The twenty great ethallic stras'ls are unbrella-ing out on foremast and main, whining softly as they swivel to catch a brisk night wind. Engines coughing. These early ships make little if any of the sounds of a sea vessel, yet they fill the atmos with their noise. Later that must hush, when hunting. The wash and rush of air across the bows isn't unlike, perhaps, the thicker splash of waters.

Maud is by the rail on the main deck and adds up the number of the crew. Only twelve men are needed for such a ship; McCloud's has eleven. Maud knows that on the last night, when he and the ship vanished, he had no crew at all. This then is not the last night. But if so, there should be one man more. The names of his crew were not recorded (lax times). She has read though McCloud himself was well able to raft and use a harper's iron with great skill. Would a twelfth man be redundant?

He stands on the bridge, and Maud looks up and studies him. That the other sailors see her is unlikely. That is, they won't see her as anything unusual, mistaking her, (fore-brain coining a quite customary – if wrong – assessment that she's a part of the ship's furniture, or one of themselves, or a reflection or optical illusion). There may not anyway be even a rudimentary consciousness left in these shadow-figures, who irresistibly, and non-professionally, remind her of the phantom crew of Coleridge's *Ancient Mariner*. They look mostly solid, but never entirely finite. Her eyes slide off *their* faces as theirs, if they *are* at all aware, will off hers. Sometimes 'ghosts' like these, which are only a replay of former action, do come with a wisp of awareness. Like a flicker of stray electricity crossing a dead LT screen.

But he, McCloud, is NAATH. He *is* aware. His type of ghost is neither a recording nor an impulse. It's a fragment of the human being, left stranded by trauma in a sentient world. (It is this of *him* that invests the ship, and makes her also dangerous).

Here in his mind-recreated past, he looks as real as living Jenx and Apharis. Much more so, to Maud Ruby, as she studies him. The lean face just starting to show the maturity of thirty-eight years, the arched black brows and large black eyes, whose sight is still sharp as any burny iron. His hair, black thick, long and wavy as shore-weed, is tied back, revealing a strong neck, low, broad, intelligent forehead. He has a sensual mouth, but she thinks the sensuality in him isn't necessarily sexual. He will like and have women, perhaps men, occasionally. But it's the ship and the sky and the things he hunts that have his attention now. Maud can imagine him running the unsmooth skins of his kill through battle-calloused fingers. Ballin whales feed on sky; he too in his own fashion.

Standing one instant later behind him on the bridge, she knows he continues to see and hear her. "Tell me about the whales, Captain McCloud."

"Oh, do you have a hundred years to hear that, then, Redhair?"

"I have all night."

"But I don't, you see. We've business tonight. Stay close and watch. You'll learn all you need of them, the Ballin."

She's young again. She can't not feel the excitement. She doesn't touch him, the back of his coarse-cloth coat, where the wide muscles of his shoulders show, and the play of powerful lungs, enhanced by the thin airs of upper atmos. She looks at the line of his cheekbone, the decided jaw with already returning stubble, the dense black lashes of his dark eye.

"What happens tonight?" she asks softly.

"Before? Or after?"

"So you know it," she says. And realises she talks a different way here, the rhythmic argot of old High Egypt, and the softer way of her youth. But she has never, in all her multifarious experience, confronted a 'ghost' like this one, who answers back, foresees, and culpably *joins in*.

And she says, "Both, perhaps. But now, just before, perhaps."

He tells her, without emphasis, looking only out into the now gushing torrent of splitting moon-surfed cloud. "The

Mate, Mr. Vemmer, he took sick and couldn't sail."

"Which concerns you? Are eleven men too few?"

"Never, not for me."

"Why then?"

"I know in my heart's pit – Vemmer isn't sick. He's sailing tonight aboard my wife, riding and rolling up there on the top of her and the town, in my bed on Amber Street."

Despite their resemblance to a phantom crew, McCloud's ten men work efficiently, just as they must have when alive.

The other harper (harpooneer) is overseeing the two sailless auto-rafts, which can move swiftly and with only the faintest phizz of noise. Each raft will carry three men besides the harper, a frontman, midman, and the lineman at the rear, who must with perfect choreography pay out the harpoons' quicksilver cords. Two rafts manned will see three men still aboard to shipkeep the mother vessel – sometimes the rafters will leave her far behind, in hunting a whale.

Maud knows all this, has read it up. But reading is one thing. She'll be in the first raft, a fifth member, if weightless and unapparent to any but McCloud. Her presence, she's entirely aware, will make no difference either way. For this now is pure replayed mnemonic recording, unchangeable though able to exaggerate.

The raft crews don their eye-shields.

The rafts are birthed like bolts from a bow.

Inside seconds they've travelled at least one hundred zers.[4] Bracers insulate from the launch-impact Maud hasn't even felt, but the men grunt dully, used to it, a ritual honoured even by their shades. And now, racing due south, deep vocal silence closes down, to keep the quarry in ignorance of their advance. Only whispers come inside the face shields, hot greedy whispers like those of people aroused and urgent for sex. But the dirty foreplay is for the Ballin.

Even *he* whispers with the rest. A kill means money –

---

[4] Zer: Approx 10th of a Kilometer

survival – a place in the world. Has he forgotten his wife, (some woman the records never even mentioned), and First Mate Vemmer, both of whom may also whisper just like this, before man and woman kick and tumble, howling with delight, in the rumpled bed?

> OLDEARTH ARCHIVE ISSUE: X2. 06911
> **BALLIN WHALES** (Ref: Z/d7)
> Valued, accordingly hunted for:
> 1) Long-life luminescent hide (providing stripped from corpse, does not rot and is low-maintenance), superior to fy-neon or mercury. Supplies non-toxic, non hyper- G.-W. lighting.
> 2) Hollow bones (use: music).
> 3) Form of ambergris (gut) (use: Medicinal: rheumatic and allied conditions. Also in jewellery).
> **Meat** – negligible. It has been estimated a single 90-foot Ballin whale supplies only the equivalent of one large earth-type turkey carcass.
> **Blubber** – none. (Oil is also insignificant.)
> **Blood** – High volatility and evaporable. Diasporous.
> (Useless.)

The hunt

They are hunting the whale.

Ballineers, oh ballineers.

But is tonight's hunt *that* tonight so long past – or some other past night of his. For a succession of vertiginous moments, the redhaired woman on McCloud's raft, (or the old woman in her cabin on *Spanish Lady*), sees a mindscape montage of images and events from earlier times. Filtered through her new and profound awareness of this man, she can identify, she judges, which persons they are that crowd his memory.

A handsome, slightly younger shipman, dark-haired too, stands under the foremast playing a whale bone fluta as the ship flies. Between breaths he grins. Pleased with everything, himself included. This surely is Vemmer, First Mate, friend, possibly also lover. Has Vemmer met McCloud's woman yet? But then he's gone, and she sees two rafts racing in a morning sky tangled with mallow cumulus, and McCloud harpoons a vast seventy-foot Ballin, the line spinning out, the air cascading with broken motion and storm. These brief pictures seem to last less than fifteen seconds. In the mind in the cabin of *Spanish Lady* probably they have taken up thirty minutes.

Then the memory-shoals clear. He's thrown them free to see if she will note them. But in the raft she doesn't speak, doesn't mean to distract him, even though presumably she can't.

And right then the lineman at the raft's stem whispers fierce enough they must all hear, "It blows!"

Sky whales also breach for air. *Downward*.

Descending from the upper atmos or higher, they spout through the blow-holes in their heads the differing vacuums or gaseous substances they've breathed in above. These spouts vary, transparent or in odd colours, (saturnine ochre, orange, alabaster white), and sometimes with stinking or perfumed odours. Harpers 'stung' by such a discharge have been known to become inebriated, pass out or puke.

Tonight's blows are still far enough off, and watery, with a vague taint like rust. The pod comprises eight in number. Now their tails swirl the mooney cirrus. "Flukes!" sighs the whispery lineman, and stands ready as McCloud seizes up an iron.

The biggest of the whales appears. Maud thinks it looks at them with its small sidelong eye. The genitals are sheathed; Maud isn't sure if the animal is female or male. But it's a good eighty feet, and the others in the pod, now cloud-splashing and diving as they suck the sub-mesopheric air, are much less. The big whale is the prize. The wels[5] of its bluish-magenta envelope are crusted with tropian barnacles, and scabbed from some fresh quarrel – undoubtedly not with Ballinkind, but most likely some careless human craft. This doesn't mar the

---

[5] Wel: Measure for whaleskin, approx 4 metres

creature's magnificence. For how gorgeous it is, swimming and unfurling its vast atomic-explosion-shape of tail, that smashes the moonlight like the waters of the deepest sea.

They're near enough now the whale has noted them. It shows no alarm. They haven't seemed to learn, these pacific leviathans, that men mean harm. Curious, for in other ways Ballins are highly intelligent.

The raft jumps. No one can be dislodged; the magnetic bracers hold every physical thing aboard.

McCloud's standing for'ard, leaning out. The athletic pose is statue-like, extremely pleasing to the eye. He casts the harp-iron unerringly and the lineman responds like another muscle in McCloud's body, paying out the frizzled dazzle of the line.

Straight in behind the slope of head the blazing point runs home.

That doesn't kill, it holds.

Now the raft has *fastened*.

The rest of the pod veers away. It's as if they don't understand, as humans often don't when one of their number is attacked in front of them. What makes men stare and stand aside isn't always solipsistic cruelty, cowardice or brainlessness. It can be mere shock. The dual barrier of personal isolation and personal connectedness to others, staggers – is it *I* who has fallen? If not, how can it fall? The bell tolls for all. We stare motionless at the bell.

McCloud casts in a second iron.

These lines don't break, save in an extraordinary flurry, unless laser-severed.

There is a third lung, up behind the head. It's this which washes out the alternate atmoses from the two larger and lower lungs. And this tertiary lung, not the heart, is the only truly vulnerable place: the Life.

Yet first comes the *gallop*. Line-attached to the panicked, furious and now-plunging whale, a raft must ride behind it as it speeds away.

And so, as the whale rushes forward, trying to outrun the

fate already clamped fast in its body, McCloud's raft springs after. They *gallop*, like a silver kite at the mercy of a redly violet storm.

> *God help a world that was so ill-designed,*
> *That we must kill this other prince-like kind,*
> *Christ help us all – but that's to no avail –*
> *For we must live by*
> *Hunting the whale.*

Finally they caught her. (She *was* a she, as Maud saw at last.) The Captain of the *Perilune* stabbed once, twice, into the upper lung. Blood flew out of lung and blow-hole like crimson stars, like scarlet birds, all ruby red, and stained the fucking moons. But of course, it didn't do that. It barely stains anything. The blood of Ballin evaporates quickly on contact with oxygenated air, as in the stratosphere, to which by then the raft had descended.

They call the death dance a *Floral*. Why? Maybe for the red flowers of death. Luckily it does not take long when well-managed. Starved of true oxygen the whale's brain darkens. She faded, fainted, died inside fifteen seconds. Like... memory.

After this she lay like an island on the night (one moon down, another rising). She's a sky-beast, hollow boned, light as – a heart. Secured to the raft by harper lines, easily they could pull her back to the ship, strip her and portion her, and search the ropes of her intestines for the chance bonus of dull-gleaming gems called grey amber.

These men weren't wicked. They slew because they needed to, to pay their way and keep themselves and their kin and kind.

But what worlds. What a system. So ill-designed.

Yet old Maud, in her locked cabin of trance, didn't have another minute for any of that. Time had moved again. The kill was over.

He's leant back on the bridge rail, but looking in at her, where she stands under the sprit.

The ship is empty of anyone else. The whale from the past, that she had just witnessed them hunt and slaughter, has vanished with everything else of flesh and blood. The mindscape edit has occurred again. It's another night now. It's *that* night now, the last. But he had been alone then. In this replacing reality she is here to share it with him.

"They say these whales have no voices, but I've heard them," he says quietly, "calling in my mind, singing sweeter than their own blown bones. They're passionate, like men and women. Faithless like them, too. So we and they are the same kind in that, and in other things, and both of us live till death kills us. I kept on seeing him, Vemmer, playing that fluta bone, smiling. Light-hearted, as I never was. And that night he was in the town with her, and we took the first whale, that other piece of the night, him and her, I never turned my mind to it. I thought I could still be what I was. Then came the *other* whale, out of True North, black as tar and near on one hundred feet. Two giants in a night. I was always proud, Redhair, of my ship and my skill. I never killed a Ballin but swift and clean. Oh, I've seen plenty make a hash of it, and the whale slow-stifling, dancing floral around and around for twenty minutes and more, and the whole sky sopped in blood. But never from me. Never Captain McCloud. Even that night, when I knew *he* was at her – and *she* at *him*, I went on to take the second whale."

He stops. He gazes at her. Maud says, in her young, softer way, "And did you manage it, Lir McCloud?"

"Christ help me," he says.

Maud's familiar with the various pieties revived on the New Planets. But this is less prayer than preface.

She waits. He tells her.

What she has seen already during the first hunt, chase, harpooning, gallop, were once more created, now by his voice only. The harpoons went in flawless. The second raft too fastened. But as usual it was McCloud who swung solo to wield the lance and take the Life.

As he boasted, and as his crew had boasted of him, he never made a mistake. But that night he did. He had thought himself focused as ever, but no. Maud could have told him, the siderooms of the brain are never unbusy, while the sly subconscious and pathological id wait in ambush. But too it wasn't always possible to be on guard against oneself. It took enough to guard against fellow humans.

The lance, instead of running straight home, nipped the tertiary lung – and stuck. It had caught there in the protective cartilage that saved a sky whale from the assaults of birds, but not, obviously, from stress-iron. McCloud, seeing at once his misjudgement, tried to slice the lance back out, out of the black whale. If he could get it free, and instantly laser off the harplines, the Ballin would escape and drop lower to the tropos. Here, washed by richer oxygens, rent tissue would heal. In the code of any decent whaleship this was what you must do after a fouled strike. A minimally foul-lanced whale, metal still in it, could live on for ten days, strangling. It was quickly too dangerous to approach in its floundering, could not be cleanly finished, suffering – and useless. Ship's guns were no good either. The animal was too large and elongate. Holed, it would suffer worse, lose directional sense, and might come down on a populated area. The only hope was to retrieve the iron, cut lines, and leave the whale to repair.

McCloud tried but failed in this back-up manoeuvre. Some freak of angle, or of the individual creature's construct, had gummed the bladed lance-tip irrevocably through bone matter and lung-case. McCloud then released himself from the bracers and attempted to climb alongside the zinging whiplash of lines and so pull out the lance. But now the Ballin was thrashing; he was dragged back by the frontman. A moment more and the raft was hit and keeled; turning upside down. Next all harpoon- lines tore out – or snapped, a rare event.

Trailing silver and scarlet the whale plunged away. And from its blow-hole spouted an upward waterfall of ominous wine.

Presently they saw the whale pitch headlong down. It had partly lost control, but was not yet heavy enough with dying blood to crash all the distance groundward.

McCloud's curses and those of the raft men went to silence. Back on *Perilune*, the shipkeeps stared in awe.

Later on, he said, he returned to the port, found Vemmer at *The Whale's Eye* and beat him to pulp. Those that didn't know thought he blamed his First Mate for absence. Those that did, said Lir McCloud would have done better to bash his own head on a wall. But by then the captain was a Jonah, that Oldearth term meaning unlucky. Not a man would sail with him.

That night of the foul-stroke, back aboard *Perilune*, he had set out to follow the injured whale. To start with his crew, crediting him still with sense and good fortune, had gone along with this.

But naturally he couldn't discover the Ballin. It was well known among all whalers that a hurt whale would conceal itself, among cumulus of the junk-clouds of the tropos, always falling lower and lower as it asphyxiated. Dying animals always struggled toward the deserts, collapsing eventually among the dust dunes and mesas. Totally camouflaged then by landscape, they were nearly impossible ever to locate. And though stories existed of whale-graveyards, stacked with still light-capable skin, unsplit skeletons, and heaps of gr'amber, if ever Ballin dead were happened on they were rotten, and their ivory smashed by falling to myriad splinters.

He said he hadn't sought the whale for any 'sensible or sane' reason. He had wanted to put it from its misery. He had wanted, (here he stumbled in his speech), to express regret for his crass and terrible blunder.

Perilune's search went on for several days and nights. Then five men rafted out. Then the other five. McCloud had lost his fortune, and his mind.

He went on alone thereafter. His coat by then was stained

from the port-visit and Vemmer's blood, but someone let the captain know his own Mrs. had nursed Vemmer back to health. Soon they were off planet, heading towards Andromeda.

How long in all did McCloud seek the dying whale?

"One sixteen of days. And found him too. I don't lie, you redheaded girl. Do you believe me?"

"Yes, I believe it all, Lir McCloud."

"What's your name?" unexpectedly he asks. As a man fully real might do.

"Maud."

"That's a strange name. I never heard it. It sounds like the word for *death* in Oldearth French."

"It means *strength in battle*."

Then he smiled. Which too she hadn't expected.

"But it's all a battle," he says, "and no victory. You have a fine name, Maud of the ruby red hair."

Maybe it was chance or fate, or a curse on him. He spotted the great black whale below, stretched where fallen on the peaks of mountains west of second north. Working the grav alone, he dropped *Perilune*, and came out, getting within some forty steps.

"I won't tell you how it was with him. The rocks were red – and black. He looked at me with his blank black star of an eye. And only then he died. He'd waited to show me, Maud Redhair, all I'd done to him by my blasted Goddamned error. All I had done to all of them, his kind, even at my best. So then–" McCloud says. But nothing more.

He doesn't need to say more. She knows he had lift-upped his ship again and shot her through all the ascending layers of the atmos, into open space. Unshielded and unclosed, *Perilune* had imploded then exploded, like a poisoned balloon.

Does he recall he has done this? Does he know he is dead now, lost even of himself? Does he understand that only this ghost, this NAATH, remains of him, still searching – but for God knows what – and death unsatisfied.

He is tied only to these places, can go nowhere else. But the

IRS came with their rescue ships, and they move the whales away where he can't go. Knowing the whale is dead, knowing that for him it never can be, only forever dying, he has tried to stop the rescue in fear he will miss the great black Ballin – even though he always *must* miss it. And for that he lashes out at the ships. And for this he will never be at peace.

In a whisper like the rafting ballineer, Maud says, "If he lived, and you could find him again."

"Then he could kill *me*," says Lir McCloud, soft now as she. "Quick or slow as he liked, and as I owe him and them all. Slow or quick. Whatever he'd have."

4. Grey Amber

Jonah down whale-belly, he calls out his gal:
Darlin git my dimer!
But Darlin answers n 'bother me,
You in the belly of a whale—
Ifn I feed ya—I feed him—
Forgit your dinner, Jonah!

Life should be more simple. Or else more complex and in more important ways.

I said I ceased to fall in love when I was sixty-two, and by seventy I was free of that exciting ailment. This stays true. But then, back in the mind-escape of forty-five years earlier, I was twenty-five again. And I did fall in love. With Lir McCloud, as may be obvious enough, I guess. He wasn't any stand-in *en passant* son or nephew, not he. He was all the things the lover is – my equal, my superior, my muse; wanted as lord and as slave; and wanted as the farthest brightest star, and as the only place of rest this side the grave.

And how then could I woo this man? How could I attract him, how could I make him glad and see him healed and whole? In one way alone. By giving him what I, the medium and arbiter of a mindscape could – the black whale: His death.

I knew he'd foreseen my role. How else had he arrived to meet me with that firm, unequivocal *There you are*. By appointment only. But now it must be phrased in the proper terms, not jarring the fragile sphere we inhabited, the past which wasn't real, yet was more real than anything else.

"We should go back," I said. "Over the desert. Due west of second north, where the mountains are."

"If you say," he replied again, resolute, nodding as if pleased with me.

That was all.

He took the helm-controls and *Perilune* turned her ghostly bulk through the deep dark seas of the sky.

Behind us the morning was coming, pale and smooth like a child's first skin.

The light would follow and find us.

But I stood back at the rail, and sent my mind away from me much farther, into steeper darkness, where the other ghost lingered, the one he wanted more than any woman, or any love in the world.

By the time I was old and met Apharis and Jenx, those mountains had been named, in the fashion of High Egypt City, Sphinx Ridge.

Forty-five years before, however, they towered up nameless from the mindscape, and looking down, nothing lay on them, broken and bleeding.

I heard him sigh. He said, "He isn't there."

And then, up between the jagged peaks, like a rival black sun the cloud whale came through the sky.

It was incredibly inky black, as in his descriptions. I wondered if this were because, perhaps, he recalled the Ballin as blacker than it had been. Its eyes burned too, not opaque or fiery or blue, but grey, the smoky-zircon colour of the amber sometimes found in their guts.

"Maud –" McCloud cried out to me – "Don't fear him – it's me he wants – and me he shall have."

Every time I think of this now, it makes me hesitate – that he thought to reassure me, even though he knew – as he did – I could take no harm.

Oh yes, the Ballin had come for him. He had been calling to it all these decades. I had only conjured its concrete memory. Yet there were scars along its back, whitish on the sable hide, where ancient harpoons had fastened and harp-lines razored. But not a mark from any lance. From its blow-hole spouted one long shining shot, like purest water.

Then it closed in on the ship as would an anvil cloud. It brought the smell of birds and rain and smog, and next all was darkness, black within black, yet everything visible also like electric fishes in an ocean.

Far ahead of me I saw McCloud throw up his arms, as if to catch hold of, or even embrace, the whale. Then its yards of jaw undid, and its triangle teeth were shown, they too black as polished coal, and it clenched him in them like a cat might its prey, and swung him off into heaven. He never made a sound. He vanished, and the tail of the beast crashed down on *Perilune*, and cracked her amidships.

There was nothing to be nervous of personally in this. Not even the collapse and falling which came after. It was far less than in any ordinary dream of sleep.

When the dark ebbed, we were down. Wreckage lay all along Sphinx Ridge, the broken-backed ship, and Lir McCloud, also broken, yet left there still alive. Of course. It was payment, wasn't it? Cash down. He wouldn't cheat.

Mindscapers can be like gods, for what it's worth. I struck a rock and water jetted, and I gave him some in little sips. Could I touch him? Yes, that had always been an option. But I hadn't and now made slight contact. For most of his bones seemed smashed. The shadow of the whale had gone, and did not return.

Human blood is darker than a whale's, and does not vanish.

McCloud's ghost took sixteen hours to die. I judged that by the passage of the sun and moons. Time can keep exact in those places, where it has to. Sixteen hours, one for each day he searched for the Ballin before, and it lay dying, waiting on him. He didn't know me, but now and then thanked me. His pain was so awesome he said he didn't feel any, and lied. Yet sometimes he did fail to feel the pain, and then he drifted. He called me always by another name. I don't think it was hers. Or maybe it was. But he did this without anger or sorrow. He'd forgotten everything but the blessing of the cancelled debt. Then even that. One time he asked if so-and-so was well, or if the sail had stuck again. He quoted an old song, and laughed, but left off since laughing, as in the cruel ancient joke, hurt him. He passed peacefully at the end of the sixteenth hour. Not all ghosts die in that way.

And that, then –

That was what I gave my last true lover, when I was seventy going on twenty-five, and he was dead and dying, a NAATH, with the face and body and brain and heart of a man called Lir McCloud.

I'd been gone half a century. Not quite four hours.

When I came from the cabin near midnight, I assured Apharis there should be no further trouble. It seems there has not been. Now the warriors of the IRS catch and relocate sky whales unimpeded, with caring yet efficient speed. I've received several bulletins, but I'm worlds away.

I've felt very old, more ninety than seventy. That's inevitable. I'd been twenty-five, strong and fit and flexible, and ruby-haired, and rushed back into the now usual condition inside less than ten minutes. But it wasn't that, was it? No.

I saw, in a store here, a piece of Ballin grey amber, about a month after I'd been home. From Z/d7, where else? I keep it on my desk. If I kill the lights, it glows as if there's a small mercurial flame in it, and anyhow the guy in the store announced to me how wonderful it is for rheumatism, (he had noted my weight of years). I wonder if grey amber works on an aching heart? Come on, I'm old. I can be a sentimental cynic if I like.

There's a saying in High Egypt: *The sky won't listen, so complain all you like*. But the sky *can't* listen, can it; why should it try to? We speak different languages, we and the sky. And the whales, of course, make no sound.

He saw me red-haired and vital. He never knew what I really was and have again become.

I gave him the death and the peace he craved. Perhaps I gave the great whale too the vengeance it required. And only I mindscaped unscathed, and now I've told you, I'm alone. Oh, complain all you like, Maud Ruby. All you like, old girl.

The Squire's Tale

We came to a place, a barren place on the rim of the Dead Lands, where a yellowish dusk swam between the trees. The branches were black against the evening; nothing moved in the fern among tree roots. No birds sang in the red rags of withering leaves.

My lord lifted up his helm and looked about him. All the time the horses shifted beneath us, ill at ease, stirring the earth with their feet. "There is a smell here," said my lord, "the smell of a place which has been dirtied and misused. A blight has come down with the dew, and the sun drinks it up from the ground, and the stars spit it back at night." A big white moon was rising. My lord looked at it and said: "When the moon passes over this place, God knows what rises up. Come!" And quickly we spurred our mounts away, and they trembled with fear between our limbs.

As the pale eye of the moon came nearer, the evil lifted from the earth. It came mistily and like smoke, and through the trees strange shapes like fish and serpents seemed to slide. It was a wicked place. Beyond the wood was a stake such as men use to burn a witch upon, and the embers yet smouldered on a black corpse there. There was a stench that struck the air like fists.

My lord stretched out his hand and made the holy sign as he passed. But my hands were busy with my horse, who rippled and shied beneath me. I felt a pain in my loins then, a quick agony that was gone before I had even space to cry aloud. But it was hot and wounding as a sword thrust. My sister had told me there was such a pain when my lord's brother took her; but it is a maid's pain and came for no reason at a part of me I had not, being a man.

Above the place there is the road to the town, and some way on, an inn. Smoke came out of its black nostril, and the yew branch was half-dipped to show the house was almost full. But for my lord any inn will be pleased to make room, and here, we were told, the beds were without fleas, and a magic stone was hung under the lintel to ward off ill.

The landlord gave us food in a small chamber, just beyond the crowd and noise of the tavern hall, with no company save a red cat coiled before the fire. As I tended him, my lord looked up from his meat and touched the landlord on the arm.

"There was a burning, was there not, farther back along the road?"

The landlord paled and made the holy sign. "Truth," he answered. "Today."

"A man, was it?" asked my lord.

"A woman," said the landlord, "and her body is not altogether burned. The flames held off a long while, so they say, and a devil danced by her."

A pain ran round my chest like a great band then, and my lord put out his hand to steady me. They sat me in a chair, and as soon as the agony had passed, I blushed hot with shame, for this is not how a squire should conduct himself before his lord and strangers.

The landlord held the cup against my mouth, but my teeth were clenched and I could not swallow. The metal jarred on my lip.

"He will be well enough," said my lord, "when he has slept. He is too young perhaps for such long travelling."

He was always gentle with me and compassionate, and he had defended the honour of my house, even against his own brother, but these words made me more ashamed than ever. For was I not a man? They had told me I should not be a man till I had lain with a woman, but the village girls would not, and the women that I had seen in the dark doors of the town were often foul with disease and they made me afraid.

The inn quietened about midnight, and my lord went to his bed where I drew off the mail coat from him and set to polishing his sword, such as my duty was. In the cold iron of the sword I saw his brown body burn like copper, and his hair white flaxen. As he lay on the bed, he folded his arms behind his head, and watched the last reflection of torchlight die on the vaulted roof beyond the tiny window.

"Their remarkable stone on the door will keep us safe tonight," he said, laughing deep and soft. And after that he slept.

My own sleep came on me like death. I felt my heart rise beneath the flesh and knock as one mad to be free from prison. And then it grew slower and, before I slept, I felt it stop.

It was an ill sleep, dark and close, clutching with the claws of eagles. Such sleeps, men say, have no awakening. A year in a tomb I lay that night above the tavern hall, and once a white face shone in on me like a moon. Pale as thin milk it was, with great black eyes. And behind, a flame burning.

An hour before I woke, I heard the red cat singing in the tavern yard.

My lord shook me awake, gentle and rough, and went to bathe in the water they had brought up in seven ewers to our chamber. As I stripped away my shirt for fresh, for we had ridden long, fear came like an adder from the crevice of my thoughts and stung me, for my right side and my left above my rib bones had begun to swell. It was a soft swelling, but the male nipples had turned pink as a maid's.

We stayed not long at the inn. There was a commotion about the porch, where the magic stone had fallen from the lintel in the night, and smashed to fragments on the cobbled yard. Beyond the tavern, the road was blown with leaves.

It is a day's ride into the town. Without pause we journeyed it. At ebb-day we were within gates before the watch had closed them, and above the dark loom of the houses the sky blazed rosy-brazen.

The house of my lord's lord, his uncle, is fine, of timber blood-kissed with the last sun, where we knocked and were made welcome. It was many years since I last came here, and then not as a squire but as a little page, a hand higher than the great dogs. I had forgotten all that lived within, save for memories. But the huge chase-hound was splashed with grey and blind, yet he knew me and the smell of me, and came to nose my hand. His muzzle was wet and round as a pebble from the stream thrust into my palm, and then he baulked suddenly from me, as from something ill, and his white-stone eyes flinched as if he saw with them. He followed my lord to the fire, and never came near me after, though sometimes I called to him.

There was a girl too I had forgotten. Had I recalled her, it must have been as small and fey and thin, running and laughing and in favour with my lord's lord, though only the daughter of one of his wife's women.

And now I saw her beckon me, and remembered – though she had changed utterly and was a woman, with the face of a flower that smiled. It was her eyes made me unquiet, for there is a look a woman will get when another thing is gone. She laughed at me and took my hand.

"See how red my lord's squire is grown at the sight of me. But he is a fine man, and I am the one should blush." She led me away along the stairs, my lord left below before the fire with his family. "But I have ceased blushing," said she, "and there is the cause of it." She pointed her finger at my lord's uncle, deep in talk and unknowing. "It is a danger to be fair, is it not? There, the red sea is at high tide again." And she drew me in at the shadowy bend of the stair above the hall, where none could see, and gave me her mouth to kiss. But such a kiss as she gave me had never been mine before, and when it was done she laughed again and was gone.

Faithful my heart, but I should have been mad afire for her, finding her so willing. But I was not. Rather, I was afraid of her and, as she sat that night at dinner, kept my eyes from those of hers, so fair and knowing woman's eyes they were. I was in discomfort too, for my clothes seemed all awry and would not fit me. I thought my sweat and the rain and the dry days had shrunk them.

The Squire's Tale

When the house had gone to bed, I heard her, my lord's uncle's mistress; she came scratching at the door like a cat. I had just set down the candle, and I was alone. She scratched at the door until I opened it.

"Love," she said, "I hear you sing to my lord sweetly. Sing sweetly to me."

"You will have me wake the whole house," I answered her, but she had come into the room with me, and the door swung softly to.

"Your clothes are all misshapen on you," said she. "Shame to my lord that they are."

And she thrust her hand within the lip of my doublet, as if to see how fast my heart might beat for her, which had grown dead and still.

Then the smile was gone from her face, the speech from her mouth, her hand leaped away from me as though there were poison on my flesh.

She said nothing. But something spoke in her throat, saying nothing. Her eyes were wide. Turning her head, she spat and fled from the chamber.

A shield hung on the wall. I looked in it, and now I saw the pale girl's face, the white smooth throat, and there, below the open neck of cloth, the milky roundness, and I tore wide my doublet with my hands.

The breath of life had gone from me, and still I lived, and there she lived, in the shield before me on the wall. A woman with her hair lopped short as a boy's, and the three white moons of breasts and face gleaming in the candle-shade.

My lord was gone to mass that dawn, and left me sleeping, out of kindness, that should have been beside him,

From the great stair I saw the hall, and the women at breakfast. And there the girl sat, who was my lord's uncle's harlot, wan and silent, the other maids laughing and trying to tempt her with a bowl of honey and milk. She would not eat and, as her eyes lifted, she saw me, and she shrank away. Beneath the board, I saw her hand move in the holy sign.

Like a leaf blowing, the thought came and led me, and I turned my back on them and went from the house. The streets were bright with frost.

My cloak was about me. I hid in its muffle from the crowds. I came to the market-place, and a gypsy called to me.

"Here, see, fair one – these will win your lord's favour."

She was a huge woman, rust red, dangling two golden coils such as maids wear in their ears. I would have pulled back, but she gripped my arm.

"Lovesick, you are. I see it in your face. Give me a coin for the earrings and I will tell you how it will go for you."

I struggled, but she had me fast as fate. She pushed back the hood from my head and round my cheeks I felt the hair fall, long and soft, a woman's hair, never shorn.,

"Fine hair," she said, "summer hair. These earrings will love such hair."

After a minute her face grew darker, a cloud on fire. "Listen, young mistress, there are some will ask why a maid has on man's clothes." Her fingers bit my arm, and they taught me how it should be, for I sunk my teeth in her hand and she let me go, cursing. But there was blood in my mouth before she did.

Then I ran. Houses loomed and faded like ghosts in a nightmare, and once there was a bridge over green water where a white-faced girl looked up at me. Now the true terror came. A doorway and the spice of incense. I stood at the porch of a church, and saw far off the soft light of candles and lovely windows with the cold sky behind. How I longed then to run into that echoing gentle womb, and fall down before the altar, and call out loud to the angels and the Saviour to give me peace. But the sweet good smell drove me back, and I slunk away and vomited like a dog at the guttering.

Night fell soon after. There was no time in that place. Lamps were behind the shutters of windows as I passed. A lean dog howled dismally from some hidden yard.

As I walked, I heard the ash wind rustle at my feet and

smelled the almond smell of burning. All around, from shapeless walls, faces of imagination peered at me. I sensed the beat of a great heart thundering through the town, which only I could hear, and through the doors and solid timbered houses I saw with a third eye. Families at a meal, children and dogs sprawling in firelight, a cream jug overturned, an old man dying, and once, two lovers moaning on a bed.

On the ground too I saw, and above my head, small things, little creatures moving and living, specks fluttering between the rooftops and the stars. I was both man and woman as I walked. Man below the scar of birth, hard and stirring, and woman above, milk-white and swan-soft, and, at the join, the ripple of snake's skin, fish's scale. My fear had been vomited forth. A new sensation had come on me, jealous of its place, denying all others.

It was the mid of night that I came to the door of my lord's uncle's house. The bolt was drawn and the porter asleep, but within I heard the old blind hound stir in his ease and whine. I tapped with my fingers lightly on the shutters and they flew wide, and softly I called in to them that my lord's squire was returned, and I smiled at my words. A wretched servant in bedclothes came then to let me in, my hood pulled close about my head, and shivered as I passed for the cold wind came in at my back from the street.

I was deaf to her scolding and made my way above stairs. Soon I came to the harlot's door, and through it I saw her lying in her white sleep. I lifted the door latch then, and went in and, as I came near her, she tossed and whimpered without waking. I drew back the covers to look at her, a thing carved out of marble, like myself, but she had the loins of a woman.

She woke when the air struck cold on her body, and she lay before me dumb with fear, her eyes wide and fixed as glass. And then she shut her eyes and began to pray, and so I left her.

I crept to the door of my chamber, looking for the dark. But in the grate a fire blazed, and before the fire stood my lord. As I entered, he lifted his head and, seeing only a shadow, called to me as his squire.

Then the fire caught me, and he stilled. All the woman's hair was about my face, and in the shield I saw for a moment how womanly the face had grown, dark eyed and small jawed. The man and the snake and the fish were hidden.

"Who are you?" he said, quiet almost as silence.

I made him no answer but pointed to the fire. And when he looked, his face grew white and he seized me and, dragging the silver cross from within his shirt, he pressed it on my throat. Such a fear came on me then as I had never known. The silver burned like ice and from its four arms a numbing chill rushed into my body. But, with the four strengths in me, I beat it away, and heard it fall, and turning, fled from the house through the closed door into the night.

The dawn came pale, with the dripping of the dew, and the watch made haste to open the gates for me, for I made my voice deep, and the badge of my lord's house was yet on my doublet.

It is a steep climb at first, and a day's journey for a mounted man, so I thought it would take me far longer. But about afternoon, a dull yellow light came down from the sky, and I heard the creaking of the twisted trees as they swung in the wind. The inn was locked against the dim dusk, but from an upper window I thought I saw a white face look out and vanish at a glimpse of me.

The black trees stretched away, bare and leaden, their sodden leaves rotting underfoot. A small ragged child came wandering by, with an armful of brittle twigs. I called to him, for he did not seem to see me, and he looked up with an idiot's face. The wind blew back my hood then, and washed through my hair. The child opened his mouth and gave a thin high scream and, dropping all the wood he had so carefully gathered, tumbled away.

Beyond the wood was a stake, such as men use to burn a witch upon, but no proof of that burning remained now, no dead flesh or black bone.

It is hard to be rid of me, good people.

Tan

All afternoon she lay, her pale body soaking up the sun on the hill. It was July, and hot, and she had always tanned easily – when she could make time for it. Where sunlamps turned her yellow, genuine light dyed her golden.

She had been very careful to select a venue that was utterly private. No one lived inside six miles. The woods began at least one mile below. Here there wasn't a tree or bush. Only the mat of flattened summer grass to lie in. She knotted up her hair as well, before slipping off her clothes. The tan had to be perfect. Tonight he was taking her to the special club, to drink champagne cocktails and dance. She had had the dress two weeks. It was sheer black, sleeveless yet fairly modest from the front, though fitting her closely. But the back dipped low. She had a good body, and he liked it a lot. When brown, (gold) she would *shine*.

The place – the hill – she had known about since her youth, all of five years before. She had come up there once or twice, driven in a boyfriend's car. But others sometimes came there as well, then for different reasons. The hill was a favourite from which to spot UFOs. She herself didn't believe in flying saucers, or if there were any, why on earth (ha!) would they come near earth? One of her evening companions on the hill did point out a moving light above. But she told him it must be a plane. After she had grown up and gone away to get rich in the city, she heard that on a cloudy November night, a strange fiery object had been seen falling on the hill top. The crash and flash, the local newspapers had reported, had been heard, felt and seen across ten counties. But when police, ambulance and fire crew finally made it up the hill, nothing was to be found. "It was as if," one agitated witness later announced, "the doomed craft plunged straight through the fabric of the ground, alter-dimensionally leaving barely any evidence of its doubtless terminal descent."

The hill, now designated the 'Tomb of Unknown Friends from Another World', had for a while been much SF-geeked over. But no longer. Indeed, people seemed now to avoid the place.

About two o'clock, satisfied with her frontal tones, she turned over onto her face. She knew that in this position she might fall asleep, so prudently set the alarm on her phone for four. By then she would be the cake that angels baked.

She wasn't wrong about sleeping. After ten minutes she began to doze. She let go and slid down into a warm oblivion, where only once a peculiar dream half woke her, but afterwards she couldn't really recall why. It had something to do with crying voices, she thought, when the alarm fully roused her. Voices – and someone reaching out to her. It was not a pleasant dream. It had a sort of edge of panic to it, a weird, ill-defined frisson of resentful anger, and pain.

She shook it off quickly, of course, and by the time she was down the hill and driving back to town, she had thoughts only for the way he was going to look at her when she showed herself to him in the new dress and the new tan.

He arrived a little too early. She liked his eagerness, but would have preferred she had been ready. Even so, a glimpse in the shower, before steam obscured it, had already shown her how beautifully her legs, breasts and arms had toasted. So she donned the dress and came out, and having seen his face, turned slowly around to show him the back of her. Though she hadn't yet seen herself like this, she could well imagine. She anticipated his speechlessness, or extreme praise, perhaps even an interruption before she could finish her make-up. The one thing she did *not* expect was –

"Why are you laughing?" she demanded, spinning to confront him, startled and, well, frankly unnerved.

"God, you haven't seen, have you? What did you do, fall

asleep under a *tree*?"

"What – do you mean?" She stared at him. "Obviously I would never try to tan under a tree –"

Briskly – she had never liked his *briskness* – he directed her to return into the bedroom. "Get a mirror and take a look at your back. God!" He laughed again. "You're dumb. Go on, go and see. And then change your bloody dress, for God's sake."

She went into the other room and slammed the door. She took off the dress and grabbed a hand mirror. Standing with her back to the long mirror on the wall, she looked to see what he had found fault with. Until that minute she was thinking he had either gone mad, or was winding her up because he secretly disliked her.

In the mirror then. In the mirror.

Her back was a canvas of flawless golden flesh, across which there spread, where the sun had been statically blocked off from her for two solid hours, a lattice-work of white, untanned skin. This clearly depicted a tangle of stretching, clawing, agonized, terrified and pleading, tiny little three-fingered hands.

Thuvia Made of Mars
(Spilt Milk)

I

I think the cat saw her first. Sybil had always been rather psychic.

Since we got together, she and I, Sybil and Alma, Alma and Sybil, then youngish independent bachelor girls, I'd now and then been aware that Sybil would notice something (or other) I couldn't see at all. They always say it's a tiny insect, don't they, but no, it never was, and my own eyesight so far has always been pretty sharp. Actually, anyway, Sybil was unintentionally polite with insects, especially the little ones. Even birds, though they did interest her visually, she never pursued. I'm afraid she was a mouse-enthusiast. But she had her nights on the tiles back then, and so did I. She'd hunt, and also fight with every sparky male cat in the vicinity – always winning, too. And I, well I'd do something a little more male-friendly and relaxing, shall I say. But we both kept all that out of the flat. And then we moved into our Country House.

Sybil, by the time of the move, was getting on a bit. Me too. Years-wise I was in my latest forties, but Sybil, of course, at just over nineteen, was around ninety-eight. Where I'd thickened a little, and become a white-hot-furnace blonde, she had thinned a touch, and her dark tabby fur was a shade darker. Her eyes, which in youth were pale primrose, had intensified to a swarthy, piratical gold. I looked good. But Sybil had stayed stunning.

My unknown, never-met, just-deceased cousin had left me the house, out of the blue. Financially, it was a godsend, and otherwise rather nice, though not very big, (bigger though than the flat). It lay on the edge of a pleasant Kent town, and had an excellent if rather overgrown garden, with hilly woods around, hiding the convenient and not too active by-road that got me into 'civilisation' when needed. Also a gardener presented himself about a fortnight after we moved in. He had the illustrious name of Bellringer. An oldish guy, but hale and tanned and strong.

He had worked – if only about five times a year – on my cousin's garden, and she had recommended him to the solicitor.

Sybil at once came up to give the gardener a check.

He too responded immediately. He bent and stroked her, ably and appreciatively. She gave a purr and winked at him. She only ever fought male *cats*, (still did if not prevented), not male humans.

The deal was struck, friendly, easy.

I found the grave in the garden after Bellringer's first efficient mowing and shrub-tidying visit.

"Do you know anything about this?"

Bellringer gazed down at the tiny mound, with its equally miniature moss-greened stone.

"Mmm," he said.

"*Thuvia*," I said. "Was it a pet someone buried? That's odd. I didn't think my cousin had any."

"No," he said, "she didn't. But it's before her time. 1950's, that is."

Sybil by then had gone off on her own post-mow forage.

He and I stood mutely, and I had a horrible image – maybe this was the grave of a baby, unlawfully hidden here.

Bellringer seemed abruptly to sense my unease.

"There's nothing in there," he said, "that was ever living. A child put it there. A toy she loved."

Thuvia. I knew the name, couldn't think.

Then it came to me.

Whatever had been buried under the rhododendron, was named for a character in one of Edgar Rice Burroughs' science fiction tales. Mostly renowned for his novels of Tarzan, Burroughs also penned some very engaging stuff set on the planet Mars, starring the redoubtable John Carter, and with wonderful female names such as Deja Thoris, or *Thuvia, Maid of Mars*. When young, in the '70's, I'd read some and liked them a lot. But I'd also later heard the inevitable joke – *Made* replacing *Maid*. I'm afraid I laughed. I was a fan of the chocolate bars too.

Bellringer, though he'd seemed to strive to douse my uneasiness, now looked slightly embarrassed. So I changed the subject, asking him if he thought the apple tree might produce new fruit.

I hadn't seen anything else unusual then. Although, as I say, I'm sure Sybil had.

Then I *did* see it - her. About two nights later.

In bed early after a really boring doing-the-chores day, I was fast asleep. Then woke up with a start. My alarm-clock showed 1.30 a.m., and Sybil, who generally lay curled up by me most of the nights, (as in fact she always had when both of us were in), was gone. I thought she'd sought the bowl of water on the upper landing, or her indoor 'emergency' litter tray. But then –

Oh my. Then.

What had I thought she'd been looking at before, those times in the long through-room downstairs, or the downstairs 'office', or cloakroom? Well certainly, something *I* couldn't make out. And as I've already admitted, I'd never in the past seen whatever it was Sybil had ever stared at, following it with her formerly primrose (now pieces-of-eight-gold) eyes. Yet tonight, in our new hall, just outside the part-open bedroom door, darted a little – *something*. It was a bit under one and a half feet tall – about half a metre in modern language. For a second I did unsurprisingly perhaps, think it was another cat. But not a cat that moved on four paws. A cat running steadily on its two hind legs –

I'd had an impression of colour, too. White, and also darker, browner, a sort of dense honey shade. And blackness flying, a long banner of thick hair...

"Sybil!" I called, absurdly. Then, when she didn't come back in, I got up, now wide awake, and went out into the narrow corridor that runs crossways here from the landing, with the four upper rooms and bathroom opening off it. No light was on, why should there be, but a clear, water-ice white three-quarter moon floated in the central back bedroom window, throwing down a shape like a transparent playing-card on the landing. And there sat Sybil, calm and watchful, and *looking*, her eyes moving to follow what she saw. Which was this small, dare I say *elphin* figure, with a honey tan and long white dress, and long black woolly curly hair, which apparition was trotting by her, and away into the shadows of my study.

I stood transfixed. As they say. Had I just seen one of the Fey Folk? A faery? Or was it – was it the tiny little Lilliputian ghost of a female being, in a white silky gown and wool hair and finely-textured *knitted* amber skin?

I wasn't scared, I remember that. I was – excited. And also somehow a little ashamed, as if I'd just caught sight of a nice old woman as her bloomers fell off – Ridiculous analogy, but I can't think of another that fits closely and correctly enough.

After another minute or two I pranced (Alma the clown) into the study and clicked on the light. Nothing. Of course.

Outside, on the landing, Sybil gave a chirrup, very like a soft knowing laugh. Then she entered the bathroom and used her litter tray, which as a rule she seldom did, preferring the great outdoors. Maybe her comment on my human crassness. Or just to show me that now *the coast was clear.*

"It's good, this," he said. "Lovely bit of cake. The wife used to make them, then she didn't. Went over to the shop-bought stuff."

"Well," I said, "when I get the time, I like making them. Now and then, you know."

I'd asked him into the quite roomy kitchen for a pot of proper black leaf tea, (no bags), in my green china pot, and a slice of the chocolate cake I'd baked for the genuine reason given above.

But obviously, I had an ulterior motive.

Meanwhile Sybil was outside, near the just-blossoming apple tree, sunning herself in a suddenly rich spring sun.

"Can I ask you something?" I said, pouring us each our second mug. "It's about that – er – grave. Thuvia."

He didn't touch the new tea, for which he'd been reaching out. He looked at me with his large, intent brown eyes.

"It was a toy, you said," said I.

"Yes. A doll."

"A doll that was loved, and so buried. But why? Dolls don't die."

He looked down, and touched a crumb of chocolate left on his plate. As if, now, he couldn't expect seconds, or even to finish the crumbs of the first.

"It did," he said, "kind of. Die. In its own way."

"Will you tell me?" I said. "You see *she*," pointing out of the window at Madame Sybil asleep below the tree, "*she* sees it all over the house. And now *I* do. A little slim brown-skinned doll with long, long black curly wool hair, and a white gown. I hope you don't think I'm lying."

No hesitation now: "I don't. I saw it once, too. Just the once. In the garden there. Thought it was a squirrel. Then I knew it never was."

"What happened? I mean, to the doll when it was – alive."

"Oh. What I heard, the kid, little girl, she loved the books, that Mr Burroughs's Thuvia story. And so an auntie, she made her a Thuvia doll. A Martian Princesss."

"A Martian doll!" I was a moment rapt with wonder. Well, how imaginative, how *wonder*-full.

"Kiddy loved her – the doll. And then, a few months after, kid's in the kitchen, and there's a big old pan of milk bubbling on the stove, and the darn pan breaks, kind of explodes. Nobody knows why. A great stream of scalding milk comes bursting out and hits the little girl in the face – only it doesn't, because she's holding Thuvia up to her face right then, kissing her, and telling her secrets, like they do. It's the doll that gets boil-soaked and scalded – ruined, can't repair it. The child just has this little burn on her shoulder, and a little one on her left hand. Marked her for years, but not serious. But if the dolly weren't there, it had been her face, and blinded."

A huge, soft, thick, glowing, heavy silence has filled the kitchen. Our tea is cooling in the mugs. The cake smiles mildly at its reflection in the green plate.

I think of what had almost been, and a sort of wrenching comes across my heart. Poor little child. Poor rescuing inadvertent doll...

"So her mum had the dolly buried, to help the kiddy with her grief, and the grave marked, too, and the kiddy used to put flowers on the grave. Till she was grown. And then she married and moved away. By then their father was dead. And the mother went to London to be with her other daughter. And your cousin took the house. *She* never saw any – well, nothing. But me, just the once – it was way back, just after my missus told me the story, I didn't work here in those days, just as I was passing, and something made me stop."

"*What* did you see, Mr Bellringer?"

"Call me Sid," he said. And then, "I saw her up a tree by a window. The dolly. It was just on twilight. When the shadows come. And there she was. This little scrap of a thing, golden Martian skin and long dark hair and her white princess dress. And her eyes. I could see them shine, like dark glass."

"Which window? Where?"

"Upstairs. Bedroom maybe."

"What else did she – the doll – Thuvia – what else did she...?"

"Nothing. She just seemed a bit sad, well, she'd be lonely. And then, she was gone."

You could imagine it, I suppose. Her ghost left here all alone. Maybe the child even forgot Thuvia, when grown up, and fallen in love with a real live human being. Not meaning to be cruel. Maybe even she said goodbye to the grave. (I remember the grave of my mother. I hardly went there. I loved her, and for me she wasn't in any grave. But Thuvia –)

I thought of Thuvia wandering through the garden, then getting into the house. And my highly practical cousin thumping about. (I had heard tales of her. I shouldn't be ungracious, and I'm madly grateful, she left me the house!) But the little ghost doll. All alone. Forever, maybe, because how long does *ghostness* last? Is it a sort of apprenticeship for the next life, or for another life *here* – only for a doll – God knows. Poor little doll. At least, as a ghost, she was dollishly still pretty, and well-dressed. Not a hint of the bloody awful exploding milk.

(I asked Sid Bellringer to call me Alma that afternoon. My mother named me after Alma Cogan, a charming and fun singer on the then-Light programme.

After that, Afternoon Tea, and Morning Coffee became a habit between us, depending on the time of day he was there. Before he'd just had tea-bag tea in a mug with some biscuits in the garden. I confess, I didn't always bake cakes though, only if in the mood.

He was, is, interesting. He knows so much about plants and gardens both obscure and famous, and about people, too. And places, other countries, cities... His wife, who sounds like a woman I'd have got on with, died eight years ago. That's sad, but it seems they were happy while they could be, and emotionally very close – 'never apart'. I never had a relationship like that, but I never aimed for one. I'm envious, but relieved.

Except, of course, with Sybil, my feline sister-in-arms. Always together, when not on our own business. Longest relationship in my life, that one.

And Sybil was very keen on Sid. She'd sit on his lap and purr. What a flirt.

But all this is, at least partly, beside the point.)
So, to continue the story of Thuvia.

I'd see her quite often, from then on, usually after full dark, once or twice in pre-dawn twilight, or the evening dusk. Never very near; perhaps she was cautious of me, or shy. And there would be gaps, a week, a fortnight even, when I didn't see her at all. I used to ask Sybil then. "How's your royal princess friend, Sibby?" Sybil, naturally, did *not* reply. But I had a strong feeling that Sybil would have shown symptoms of disturbed surprise if Thuvia had simply disappeared for good.

And there was one evening, late that summer, I recall, a hot, still, navy-blue hour just after quarter-moonrise. I was sitting on the lawn in a garden chair, looking at the stars, and wondered vaguely where Sybil had gone and what she was up to. But she was frequently off on her own errands, a part of her great charm; an independent lady, who still loved me enough to want to spend time with me, other than meals, too.

I'd had a thought, I have to confess, (an unworthy one): was Sybil so intrigued by Thuvia because my cat believed her some sort of large etheric Mouse? An unfitting idea indeed.

This evening though there was a sudden springing rush in the shrubbery by the wall. But what leapt forth was not Sybil, but a large black male cat I had seen here and there before. He was attractive and healthy and quite young, and I pondered whether he might have had a run-in with Sib. He had that look, slightly ruffled, but – having seen me – going all nonchalant, sauntering into the shadows. Oh, whatever it was, I meant to do it, said his demeanour. Always in control, *c'est moi*.

Sybil, of course, by then should not be attacking young males, at *her* age. So I went to make sure she was OK.

She was. There she lay, quietly sleeping under the apple tree, (which had pleased us so much by aspiring to produce apples soon to be picked, by Sid and me). Her sleep was so profound, her fur smoothly poured and rising and falling with gentle respiration, that I suspected she'd missed the handsome fightable biteable feline youth. About to turn and resume my stargazing, I caught a flick of pallor. And so I saw too the doll sitting there about half a foot from my cat. I *had* seen Thuvia seated before. Once, rather memorably, on the banister-head at the top of the stairs. But now all her attention – if so I can call it – seemed centred on Sybil. As a doll she had only one expression, knitted and stitched in, vague, regal. But something – how can I put it?

I thought, very oddly, of a small child with another somewhat older child, one the younger child trusts, likes, is comfortable to sit beside, even if the older child is sleeping. It wasn't as if Thuvia were *guarding* Sybil. Just – watching over. I went back to my chair, and found I had begun to hum a lullaby from way back in my earliest childhood, something my mother had sung me. *Golden Slumbers.* Silly, sweet, perfect.

Thuvia was watching over Sybil and singing her a lullaby, then? Silent and wordless, *phantasmal.* But sweet. And profoundly kind.

When I drifted in to bed around eleven thirty, I left them to it. Sybil woke me briefly when, having come in via the cat-flap, she joined me at 2 a.m., curling up by my head. She was alone, relaxed, and in turn sang her own lullaby to me, in her lovely contralto purr, that shook my pillow with its marvellous vibrato.

II

Summer had been beautiful that year, and autumn was spectacular, the woods around, and even here in the garden, having certain trees with bright red or mauvish leaves, to augment the oranges, yellows and browns. Sid knows all the names. I try to remember.

I spent Christmas day with Sid. I cooked a lavish Christmas Dinner, which we ate at 3 p.m., a time I've always observed for this traditional feast, just as once my mother and father did. (Of course, by then, Sid and I were occasional lovers. Not the passion of youth – or youth's ridiculous hang-ups and rages, thank God. Fondness and friendship, and a lot of damned fun. He's a bit older than me, but I'm no girl. We suit, and we don't crowd each other either.) Sybil liked Christmas Dinner, always had done.

She would have her own cat-size plate of turkey, even carrots and a little roast potato, cut to size. A happy time.

Next year was fine. Though the winter-spring weather was foul. Now and then Sid would come to cut the grass and be rained off, and we'd just sit and drink coffee and talk. When summer arrived the warmth was intermittent, two days on, five days off, sort of stuff. But we went for walks and to the cinema in town, and Sybil still got her siestas on the lawn on fine days, or up in the sunny back bedrooms.

Now and then I would catch sight of Thuvia. I always said hello, by this time. I spoke to her in a calm, friendly way

"Hi, Thuvia, nice to see you. Hi, Thuvia, how are you?" Why not? She took no notice, but perhaps she felt the welcoming vibes.

Sybil though was always aware of her, even when *I* didn't see Thuvia at all. I had got the impression, (aside from my irrelevant mouse comment), that my cat liked the little ghost. And, too, there were a couple of times more when I saw Thuvia sitting by Sybil, and once Sybil was then awake, and gazing back at her, calmly, herself also seated, and with paws tucked in. Sybil never, that I saw, tried to touch, to make physical contact. It wouldn't have worked. Couldn't have. Can't touch a spirit. Sad, that. I confess I too had come to like Thuvia by then. To care about her, perhaps, however hopelessly.

In a white, wind-stripped-bare end-of-October, I woke up one morning around 8 a.m., and there was nobody there. That is, Sybil *was* there. But she wasn't. Not anymore. She was dead. It must have happened gently, in her sleep. I'd kissed her goodnight around 1 a.m. – up late watching TV, and she already installed on the bed. She'd rubbed her face against mine, and returned into her slumber. Never surfaced. No disturbance. Peaceful as a slow sunset.

The white morning sun now shone in, and lit her fur like dark grey velvet. But the lamps of her eyes were shut. A single white whisker had been dropped, as sometimes they were, on the edge of the duvet. I still have it. Always shall. She was nearly twenty-one years old. In human terms, well over a hundred.

"Sid, are you all right with this?"

"Course I am. Wouldn't think you'd want her anywhere else."

I'd asked him if he would mind digging the grave for her here, in the garden.

Then I said the second thing. "I thought... maybe next to Thuvia."

He looked at me. Great eyes, Sid, sometimes dark as Guinness, and sometimes, like just then, almost copper. "Yes?"

"Well, she *saw* her. The little doll. Didn't she. And I've told you how once or twice *I* saw Thuvia sitting near her."

"That's fine," he said. He downed his tea, got up, and we went out into the cold, cold, cloudy opaque day.

He dug the grave perfectly, the exact proper size. I had wrapped Sybil in a piece of old soft silvery silk. (I'd meant to have a top made from it, about twenty years before, never had.) I kissed her again and folded her in. She was curled up tight, her body hardening and lightening a little by then, a beautiful unreal case from which the content had removed. She was laid to rest, and Sid filled the grave in. I had found a smooth pale stone, and placed it on the top. I'd written her name on it, but of course this would fade. "I'll cut that for you," he said quietly, "if you'd like."

"Thank you," I said.

We stood in silence. What prayer do you say for one you love who is dead and gone and isn't human? Worse conundrum than for burying a bloody atheist. But then Sid put his arm round me and we went back in and had, at ten thirty in the morning, a whisky each.

He cut the stone – *engraved* it, no less – Sybil's name, with small elegant flourishes. One more talent I hadn't till then known he had. I didn't plant a shrub there. The rhododendron would make the show, with leaves and pink flowers. Sybil had enjoyed the rhododendron, even personally watered it now and then.

The stones shone in the dark for an evening or two after. Perhaps the disturbance of the earth caused that, or frost. *Thuvia* read one. *Sybil* read the other.

It was a filthy winter. It snowed and the snow covered everything. The wind howled over the garden, forcing the trees almost to their knees, or so it seemed. Ice hung from the drainpipes, windowsills and porch.

I didn't see Thuvia. Never. I thought, perhaps I'd done the wrong thing, asking for my cat to go into the ground beside her. Or maybe Thuvia just missed my cat, as I did, as even Sid seemed to. A gap in the safe wall of the world, where one flawless gold-eyed brick had fallen out.

I didn't, after about a week, visit the grave on purpose. Sybil wasn't there.

Spring didn't really return until May, and then, three weeks after, there arrived a full hot summer, 75 to 90 degrees (in old money). House all open windows, and during the day doors open, too.

Up from the lawn came wild flowers that I hadn't seen there before. A rose, quiescent until then, opened its magenta sculptures along the trunk of an oak tree.

It was in the dusk again, on the lawn again. I was sitting out, listening to a play on the radio, and the finches and blackbirds were paying last visits to the bird-table and birdbath we'd installed, singing presumably with beaks full of seed.

And then, along the lawn, about ten metres away, (in new money – about thirty-two feet), a small white, dark, amber form, and another, slightly bigger if not taller one, walking on four paws, tabby-grey and primrose-yellow eyed. She was young again, about five, perhaps, in human years around twenty-seven. And Thuvia too – she'd had some sort of make-over! If Sybil was sleek and groomed and full-whiskered, Thuvia's hair was now like silk, her skin smooth as good china, her dark eyes wide, bright – her dress washed, pressed and adorned with something sparkly – sequins – miniature *diamonds*?

In slow-motion, a sleep-sitter, I reached for the radio and turned it off. The play had been good. But this, oh this, was better.

"Hello, girls!" I called, a mother thrilled to insanity and trying to be urbane. "Brilliant to see you! How are you doing?"

Both of them drifted on, nearer and nearer.

My heart, like a bird, sang – and rang and ached. My eyes burned. I had the sense not to attempt to get up; I'd probably have fallen flat on my face.

When they were only about ten feet from me, they did a kind of dance together, minueting about each other, hair swirling, tail whisking, and then they had a sort of play-fight – you could see it *was* play. And Thuvia – I can't explain this – had an expression now. It was of laughter. And though I couldn't hear her laugh, through the bright sprinkles of birdsong, there was a lower vibrating note. A purr? Louder than even Sybil had managed, in life. Yet also, somehow, *soundless*.

They didn't come quite up to me. We couldn't presumably touch – except each other's inner selves, maybe. Their amused, partly condescending fond approval, my singing, ringing heart.

And then they sprang, both of them, straight up a tree.

Up, up, into the leafy higher boughs. And were gone. Or, *not* gone. Here. Real. *Alive* – in whatever non-comprehendible etheric fashion. Crazy, happy.

When I phoned Sid at ten o'clock, at which hour, if he had to work early, he might well have been sleeping, he listened carefully, and told me it was wonderful, and congratulated me.

And when I went upstairs, I wept. I cried my songster heart out. It was the first time I'd been able properly to grieve for *anyone*, because now I knew, some way or other; they would all be all right.

Lots of evenings, after that, I saw them, always together, outside the house in the garden, up trees, once on the roof playing about, and in the house too, naturally. Once they rolled all the way downstairs together. And then sprang up, not a curl or a whisker out of place.

Eventually Sid saw them too. In a way, he was bound to, they were so often about, and he, I suppose, often here after sunset. He said they were perching on the top of his spade, which he'd left stuck in the earth, (both of them, and somehow they fitted), like two robins. It was the spade for digging up weeds and so on; also the spade that had dug the grave for Sybil's body.

But why should that matter? She *had* a body now, young, and at maximum capacity.

Both Sid and I jointly saw them one hot summer midnight, when we were strolling and canoodling under the trees, and both cat and doll were there, asleep as it were in each other's arms.

He and I, together, noted that Thuvia could now close her eyes, for closed they were by eyelashed lids. Only Sybil opened hers for a second or so, winked at us, and shut them once again to sleep the just sleep of the ghost.

The summer flowed away. The autumn entered and departed. Winter was back, an unwelcome guest, bringing Christmas quickly in, like a sumptuous present to placate the reluctant hosts.

I think perhaps we were beginning to see Sybil and Thuvia, Thuvia and Sybil, just a little less.

At New Year we toasted them in champagne. A cup of

kindness. Old Acquaintance. Auld Lang Syne.

But I was the one that saw them last. Or, shall I say, for the last time in *this* world.

Unlike the previous year, there was one of those forward springs, seventy-five to eighty degrees at the end of February, and buds and crocuses and daffs out all over. The sky by day was blue as hyacinth, with transparent occasional flocks of clouds which, when the sun set around five thirty, melted into rosy embers.

I was sitting, chairless, on the lawn, in fact, and the blackbirds were already giving their sentry alarms of *Keep off, I'm nesting*. A dragonfly, green as glass, flitted past on what seemed like foot-long wings. And next, there were Syb and Thuve, up the oak tree, among the hopeful dabs of returning leaves and roses. It was very early for my girls, I remember thinking. Usually they only seemed to be around once the sun was mostly sunk – the generally accepted ghost-hours.

Half involuntarily I waved. And – to my astonishment at such a direct response – a little stiffly, Thuvia waved back.

(And she had fingers – had she had those before?) *I must tell Sid* – my first thought. But presently there would be more to tell.

They sat, and I sat, they in the gods upstairs in the tree, I in the lawn-stalls below, as the afternoon ended its drama and the curtain fell.

The sun was powdered away. The afterglow beamed and faded. Twilight came. And deepest, moonless, starriest night.

I was lying on the lawn by then, a cushion behind my head. I was idly considering getting a glass of wine and an apple – but an interruption (if you can call it that) occurred.

Like the dragonfly before, Sybil and Thuvia were suddenly whirring round and round the tree. They were flying, but without wings. I watched, admiringly. Then they dipped, and came over the lawn, passing low above me, so I saw the underside of Sybil's black/pink paws, and the little satiny shoes on Thuvia's feet. A fly-past. A salute?

After which, as before, up and up they bolted, but not now into the top storeys of a tree. This was more like a pair of rockets: they were clearly aiming at the open sky.

I'd sat up again, shot up, really. I stared after them, that flit of white and brown and grey, a double single entity – *Ascending*. Themselves two shooting stars in tandem, but not falling to earth. Falling upward into the air.

I knew, without knowing, or understanding. I *knew*.

I believed it was Sybil who coined or grasped the plan, and taught it to Thuvia. For a *made* (knitted) being, even one as imbued with spirit as Thuvia must have become, no doubt it would be harder to envisage, let alone independently accomplish. So Sybil, who instinctively predicted other possibilities, had broached the scheme, and next led them.

Up, and up.

Once or twice, lying down outside, I've felt that supernatural tug towards the sky. Yes, even stone-cold sober. (And I don't use drugs.) To leave the physical body, to lift and float and drift. To consign oneself to some other powerful, omnipresent and uncruel force. To reach some otherwhere. Some otherwhen.

I watched as gradually their small shining images melted, like the sunset clouds, into the dark and gleam of night. Until they were like feathers, and then like minute dots, and then invisible.

Not for one moment did I believe they would, now, ever return. Except, conceivably, into other reincarnated lives, a cat, a doll, or – or something else.

I lay on the still-warm grass, and saw the sown-diamond field of stars, and asked myself, less sad than wistful, *where* exactly Sybil had guided them.

I woke at 3 a.m. when the morning-night had grown cool and damp, and foxes were padding through the woods with urgent screams of volunteering lust.

To bed I took myself. Then lay awake. I wasn't, as I say, sad. It had been too beautiful, for that. I didn't know what I was.

Sid arrived at nine. He was going to see to the garden and then we were driving into town to have lunch and watch a film. I was up, ready. I didn't tell him till the coffee-break.

"All the stars were out," I said, "I could see them so vividly, and the planets – no moon, they had the sky to themselves. The stars, and Sybil and Thuvia."

We held hands and the coffee got cold. Holding hands was much better than coffee.

After a while I said, "Sid, where do you think they went? I mean, Heaven's only up there metaphorically. It just *looks* as if it ought to be. Where did they go? Eternity–?"

Sid smiled. He has a great smile. Even now, some years later, some years after Sybil and Thuvia left us, when we walk our handsome dog, Harry, Sid smiles at somebody we meet, and you can see them, especially the older women, react.

Sid smiled, and held my hand. And then he grinned. "P'raps, maybe," he said, "Mars...?"

The Winter Ghosts

Winter is a ghost that haunts the world. You know it by its grey transparencies, its crystalline white comings and goings.

It was early in the winter that I went to the town to see about some business for my Father, and was told I must call in on my Aunt. I resisted. "She has been good to you, young man," they said. She had paid for my education, and other things. My life was full of obligations, it seemed to me, and nowhere was I free to do what I wanted. I had been the slave of my school, and now was my Father's, working in his shop, where I did not want to be, and trapped in the village of my birth. I had seen and done nothing. But there again, what would I have chosen to do? I had no great driving talents. I liked to read and to lie a-bed, for either of which occupations there was now slight time. Every day I was up at dawn, for on Sunday I must go to church to show my respect to God. At night I ate my supper and fell between my sheets exhausted. What a life. The town and the prospect of visiting it had cheered me a little, despite the winter road and the stubborn old horse, the wayside packed by forest, starving beggars who seemed to signal from every glassy bush, according to rumour, and the first waves of wolves that I hated and feared along with everyone else. But now my sojourn in the town was to be divided between my Father's commission and my Aunt's fancy. It was decided; I was not to stay overnight at the inn, but at my Aunt's house. My heart sank into the floor, it stayed there, and I left it behind.

The ride was not too bad. A faint flurry of snow disturbed the horse, who for a mile kept stopping and shaking his head distractedly. I saw no beggars, and no wolves, though once I heard one howling. I arrived at the town gates before the sun set on a grey thick sky. I should proceed at once to the Aunt's, attending to my Father's wants in the morning.

I had not seen either the town or the Aunt since childhood. Both had been different then, more interesting to me. I had half anticipated some sense of purpose or festivity in the town, and there was none I could perceive; the shops blinkered, the populace running homeward before the cold. Hardly a soul on the streets. The inn looked welcoming with its gold and red sign, but now I was not going there.

What did I remember of the Aunt?

She had been slender and excitable, with a high hot colour in her cheeks. Her dark hair was drawn up with combs, and curled. She wore a dark red gown and was dancing, for it had been a festival – hence my anticipations – memories – of the town.

As a child I had liked her, but she had paid me very slight attention. Her own father was alive then, and had she not been engaged to be married? There was some tragedy or scandal never spoken of to me. Her money had come to her with the town house, at my Grandfather's death; my Father benefited in other ways. My Aunt was then alone in the world. Having no one on whom to squander the excess of her small riches, she made provision for me and my two sisters. In me, a less grateful wretch she could not have hoped to find. Far better I had liked the little drummer doll with his bells, the first gift she gave me indifferently at the festival. That was fifteen years ago. She would be old now, for she was not young then.

I reached her house, which stood to the side just off from the square. Ancient black trees, already edged with snow, occluded its walls. The shutters were fastened, and not a light showed. The house might have been deserted, the impression it gave. I dismounted, secured my horse, and tried the cumbersome knocker.

I had knocked some six or seven times before I got any answer. And then to my surprise it was the Aunt who had come to the door and opened it.

"Old Ermine died," said she, standing in the dim hall, which just barely fluttered at her lamp. "Now I'm my own maid. My own housekeeper, too. You mustn't expect too much," she added, as if we had been speaking for an hour.

It seemed she knew me, for who else but the looked-for nephew would call on her? Nevertheless I introduced myself politely, and then she extended her dry powdered cheek for my kiss. She was indeed as aged as I had feared, a skinny old woman in a wrinkled reddish dress, with eardrops of dull pearl, which perhaps she had put on to honour my advent. She wore no rings, but her hands had been mutilated by rheumatism. She led me in.

It transpired there was still an antiquated man, Pers, she called him, who would see to my horse, as he saw to the fire in the parlour, and other manly work. I caught a glimpse of him, about a hundred he looked, but the horse was getting on too, they would be patient with each other.

The parlour was like home: Crowded by slabs of the furniture, which was all I knew, and that spelled affluence, and entrapment, had I given them names. Crystal and china, perhaps never used, bulged upon a wooden mountain, dully catching the firelight through their dust. The fire was a poor one – what else could you expect of Pers?

"Will you take some tea?"

I doubted there was a drop of spirit in the house, and felt a very real and unjust anger at her, my Aunt, forcing me here to this cage, uncomfortably not equipped to please me in the least.

We had tea, and some thin jam, and she told me I should not smoke, not in the rooms. I had guessed and not tried – truth to tell, I was not much of a smoker, though it was expected in a man, a sort of condoned vice.

By now it was night, these unshuttered back windows very black beyond the rusty curtains. In the town a few panes were alight, but they looked dim and parsimonious. My Aunt had lit two lamps, these windows of hers would have that look.

I forget properly what we spoke of. There were long silences; what could she expect? She asked me of my work, which I disliked, of my school, which she had provided and I hated. She asked of my uninteresting family, and my sisters, one of whom was now married to a fat bumpkin very suitable to her.

Finally, in a sort of sneering pity, I said, "I remember you dancing in a red dress. You gave me a doll with bells. I was very young."

"Ah, that was another time." She added, obscurely. "Another woman."

Later we went into the dining room. And I had my first shock.

The long old table was hung with a lace cloth over mulberry velvet, and meticulously laid with china and a silver service. There were ten places, each fully set.

"I thought we dined alone, Aunt?"

"I never dine alone. But then again, you will see no one besides me. I, of course... I see them all. In my imagination, you understand."

Pers brought in the dishes, there were only three; they had come from an obliging cook shop, heated up in the kitchen below, but not sufficiently. Water was served with the meal. Very proper.

I was interested to see Pers pass every plate from the eight other settings. On to each was placed by my Aunt a tiny portion of the frugal meal. Pers filled each goblet from the water jug. I looked on, and tried to picture ghostly fingers raising the glasses, invisible hands plying the knives and forks. Pers left us.

"Who is here, Aunt? Won't you tell me?" I inquired, because I was so very bored, a leadenness had stayed with me compounded of snow, tiredness, inertia. Besides how could her secret guests be a hidden matter when she paraded them?

But she was reticent.

"People of my past."

"Is Grandfather there?"

"Grandfather? Of course. It is a family table. He is at the

table's head."

"Your fiancé, too?"

But she lowered her scaly eyes and would not answer. I had been indecorous, probably.

"Why did you never marry, Aunt?" I demanded brutally

"It was a long time ago."

"I recall everything well. I recall the man –" I did not – "dancing with you downstairs."

"No, no," she said.

But I was irked enough I did not allow her any rights to pain. She had interfered in my life, it seemed to me, and made things worse. She had forced me here when I might have drunk brandy at the inn. "Surely you can tell me? I've only heard stories of it –"

"What stories?"

"That he jilted you. Left you almost at the altar –"

"Oh the liars! Who said this?" She was inflamed now, surprising me a little.

"Servants – an old nurse I had –"

"None of it is true. He died. He wasn't young. His health wasn't good. The excitement... He took a chill and was dead in a week."

There was the longest silence yet.

"But you see him here tonight?" I even shocked myself at my grossness. Perhaps the water had made me drunk, I was used to a glass of wine at home.

At last she spoke to me. "Yes. I see them all. I invite them here. Why shouldn't you know? My father, my betrothed. My mother takes her place. And my mother's two sisters. Then there is my girlhood friend I see, there. She died so young. She is the youngest among us. And there is my tutor, whom I feared and loved, and who darts me terrible stern glances, because he thinks I have forgotten my lessons. And he's right in that, for I have. And old Ermine is with us too, now. I included her a month after her death, for she required her rest before that..."

A nasty but interesting idea came over me that I could see them after all. The Grandfather as I recalled him with his fob watch and high collar, the invented mother I had never myself witnessed, and her aged crone sisters in their black and lace and old-fashioned hair. The young friend caught fast for ever – perhaps she did not mind – I put her in an antique gown. The mature bridegroom, coughing a touch at his handkerchief. The elderly tutor. And old Ermine, who once or twice I had really seen, for she had been mercilessly sent to the village on my Aunt's errands when only a trace younger. I guessed Ermine was content, to sit at last at her mistress' table, even to the tepid meat and water.

"Pray don't let me prevent you," I said, "conversing with them all, if that's how you usually go on."

"You think me very eccentric," said my Aunt. "But those who are dear to me – those for whom I have a responsibility. What else should I do?"

As she had put me through the school, just so she kept these by her, these withered flowers, her ghostly dinner guests. For ever, or until her death, and – why not? – maybe beyond her death, they would sit nightly at this drab table, eat the unpalatable food – I was becoming as foolish as she.

"Well you must do as you think fit, Aunt. And now I thank you for this meal, but ask you to excuse me if I go presently to bed. The long ride tired me greatly, I'm up so early, and must be off early tomorrow, I fear, on my Father's commission."

She was startled a moment, then she settled down. The old are early to bed also, she told me, she did not keep late hours. But I must take a cup of tea with her in the parlour, to cheer me for my couch. Out of the kindness of my unkind heart I consented. I spent one further hour with her before escaping to the dusty dark room aloft. There in the great bed, by the poor light of one thin candle, I had meant to read a smuggled book.

But my own bane of tiredness came in on me. Soon the lines swam and I blew out the candle and yawned myself to oblivion.

There I dreamed of being a prisoner in my Aunt's house. I could not get out, and was in the act of bribing Pers to open a tiny door in the cellar for me – I think it did not in real life exist – when I woke. It was a milky dawn, and the fine snow blowing, and I had my Father's business to transact before I could start out on my ride home.

My Aunt was not yet risen, so I left my message of gratitude and farewell, with Pers.

The business took up half the morning, and when it was done, I gathered myself to the inn and there on top of the bread and stale tea of my hasty breakfast, I put in three brandies against the rigours of the ride home, which truth to tell I was now dreading. I had a sort of presentiment of ill luck, which drinking the brandy, rather than dispel it, had brought closer.

Shortly after midday, though it looked more like dusk, I left the town, and the staid old horse and I went down the road, and in among the great stands of the forest.

The snow had stopped, and a freezing was coming on, you felt it approach like a stealthy noise. Now and then a branch cracked in the forest at the cold, but there was no other sound save for the plodding of the horse. A faint smoke hung once in the distance from some charcoal burners. Otherwise there was no hint of any human creature. I might have been alone in the woods at the world's edge out of a legend. And this thought oppressed me, even as I began to have a quite incompatible fear of robbers.

Robbers there were, but not of the mortal type. About an hour after I had got beyond the town, when my home in my Father's house, so despised, had begun to seem to me the dearest place on earth, a small pack of wolves started to follow me.

Despite all that is said, and agreed, on wolves, they are in fact not so much of a foe to a mounted man. But I feared them and disliked them in company with anyone I could think of. My childhood had been spiced by the tales of other children the wolves had carried off and eaten, and only a dead wolf was a pleasure to see, as occasionally I had.

Their eyes were the worst, for their shapes, loping along a few yards behind me, were almost lost in the trees. But out of the afternoon dusk now and then would come a green flash, or I would see an actual eye, fastened on me with a malevolent unique intensity.

I tried a sharp shout or two, which gave them doubts, but then on they loped again. I was the only moving thing of any size for miles. They were curious, and they were hungry.

How I longed for a joint of raw meat I might have bought and thrown to them, how I longed to have drunk more, or less. Or that the old horse might have been pricked to a gallop. But my attempts to hurry him presently confused him – he did not like the wolves either, but was inclined more to congeal to stasis and shiver than to hasten off.

Perhaps they would get tired of me, and let me be.

They did not.

About mid-afternoon, when I had been followed a good hour, the old horse managed a brief canter, hit us into a low-slung bough that brought snow down on me, and stumbled. Between the bough and the stumble I went out of the saddle and slithered to the ground. As I lay there stunned, the horse, relieved of my slowing weight, gave a bright whinny and fled along the road.

I sat up before I was ready, and my head rang. Then I tried to get to my feet and slipped full length again. And then the wolves, there were five of them, came out of the trees and on to the road.

They stood looking at me, and vividly do I recollect their lean black shapes against the snow, each one exactly resembling the model of the others, as if all had been cast from a single mould of wickedness. Their eyes were like the eyes of cruel men, intent and hypnotic, yellow as flames. Was any one less than the others? An entity they were, one thing, and all gazing upon me. I despaired.

In that moment I imagined myself at the gate of death. And

this is what I saw: First the terrible rending agony of being eaten alive, and then the mildewed pit of the dead, from which a faint drear voice was calling me. "Come, dear nephew," it said, "sit down. I've laid a place for you."

And out of the teeth of wolves and shadows of the grave I emerged into that cold dining room with its table of mulberry and lace, and sat myself before a setting of dusty china and silver. To my right was an ugly young girl in an outdated gown, and to my left a balding scholar in a shabby coat. All around were old ladies with piled up fake curls, and a coughing man of sixty, and my Grandfather consulting his watch, for I had come late and kept them waiting. And there, opposite his place, sat my Aunt in her red dress and eardrops, nodding and smiling at me, as she helped me to a bobble of cold steamed food, and Pers filled my glass with water –

"No!" I cried. "You shan't!"

And I flung myself forward at the wolves. I was shouting and roaring, and out of my pocket I had taken my wooden matches, which I struck in panic and nearly set myself alight.

Perhaps it was these brief gusts of fire, or the awful noises I made, and which I myself heard as if from a great distance, but the foremost wolf backed off. As I rushed screaming down at them, all five turned sideways into the bushes, and bolted suddenly away from me between the trees.

They were gone.

For some minutes I remained, yelling and stamping, jumping up and down in the snow, while burnt matches stuck to my burnt fingers and the hole I had fired in my sleeve.

I recall I howled I would not go, I would not be caught for ever, for eternity, in that smothering. No, not I.

When I came back to my wits, no hint of the wolves lingered. A vast emptiness was there, and I was blazing hot inside the great orb of the cold. I went down the road for something to do, and found the horse loitering at the wayside a quarter mile off.

I mounted him in silence, and he walked on.

Who would believe me? I have heard since of men frightening off wolf packs with loud cries and curious behaviour, but that was in other lands, and at another time. For then I knew only I had not been brave and had best keep quiet. More than their eyes and teeth I had feared the dinner table of my Aunt, I did not want to be another of her winter ghosts. It was that cowardice which made me turn against the wolves, and, seven months later, the same cowardice which made me run away for good to another less safe, stranger, and more ordinary life.

Yesterday

Blown deserts, dry mountains, broken seas: an open untenanted sky wide as eternity. This is all that is left to us. All we are allowed.
Aside, of course, from Yesterday.

A dragon black as deep night swept slowly over the bright dawn sky, its wings star-glittering and its jaw lined with purple fire.
Below, the land was golden, its valleys dressed in green forests, the high crags rising from them, shoulders of granite dyed with the last red coral of a risen sun.
The dragon breathed a silky sigh. A wash of flame swept unsunlike in the wrong direction – down. Helpless, the earth was held in stasis. But now – there – the mauven incendiary paused – it broke and scattered, purling in exquisite rays, to form a vast sunshade. This then faded, softly as lamplight sinking in a million amethyst lamps. One must search carefully with one's eyes to solve the mystery, finally locating, on a tall up-thrust of mossy rock, an aged man, who stood firm and fearless as any mountain, even to his snow-cap of silvered hair and beard. A mage, a sorcerer: with his cunning spell he had becalmed and next put out the falling lave of fire. Even as it sank to nothing, the dragon, high in the sky, unaggrieved, perhaps even unnoticing, soared on, passing into distance until, against the tender amber screen of day, it was only tiny and unthreatening as a crow.

The three riders of the peculiar vehicle will ride on, bumping over the terrain, which is momentarily veiled with verdancy, and which next will be barren as a burnt dry crust.
In a while Linardien will say, "I shall miss them, those

dragons."

But Simyo will contradict, "The sorcerers are better."

"Were," will add Ulvad, the syntactical pedant, "*were* better."

Simyo: "For now, just for a second, they still are."

Linardien: "Look, here comes another!"

Ulvad: "Use your eyes, old darling. That's no dragon. It's a giant bird."

"Oh, so it is!"

And they will again gaze upward, as the feathery white form gushes by above, a sky-shutting storm of wings and wonder, beautiful, terrible, until it too is gone behind a crag.

Simyo will then say, "A colossal dove."

No one will argue, not even Ulvad. For this time Simyo will be quite correct.

A dead sea.

Whomsoever the traveller was, could he be indifferent to this sumptuous expanse of gleaming, dancing water? To have journeyed so long across the endless sea-green hills, but now – at last – to crest the rise and find before him the vista of an emerald infinity.

Woods, pastures, fields and lawns – to this – were as mild velvet to the wildest silk. Or, more aptly, verdigris (beautiful though it was) to jade.

And the green lived. It moved. It *breathed*.

After a while, however, the traveller became aware that not merely had liquid ocean permeated the arena of the shores, rising and falling, withdrawing, incoming – but the essence of life was also there.

Thus inevitably and soon the god of the depths rushed forth. Crowned with shells, in his chariot of green-gold drawn by dolphins, porpoises, sea-horses of great size, he rode toward some other junction of his aqueous kingdom. Who could have dared detain him?

The sea will be dead now, and approaching it Linardien, Simyo and Ulvad will look at it uneasily. Despite that, when the other image, the vastness of enormous waters filling the corroded, shelved, dry bowl – like some library of knowledge sweeping in to reveal a Past-Time of opulence and excellence – as a flowing tap must fill up a marble basin – they *will* look at it, and turn away. Though Linardien will need to wipe tears from his eyes, (water to water, earth to earth, dust to dust), and Ulvad will utter a soft and unobtrusive curse. And Simyo, bless her rebellious heart, will think: *No, no. This is not to be the only truth. I will write of this. I will sing of this. One day, please – oh, no gods remain to pray to – fuck that. Please, God, one day it will return, the sea –*

But nevertheless, the sea, by then, will be dead, the image of it already re-cancelled. No gods, no chariots, no... what will be, or what is – the word? No *soul* –

Oh – Yesterday!

Yesterday the world was full of magic. Dragons flew, lions with wings, gargantuan birds all fire. Unicorns cantered, white as ice and icing – alabaster in motion. The skies melted through cinnabar and bronze to sapphire, topaz, ruby – to ebony, black-pearl and iron set with diamonds. And an ivory moon rose, who changed her shape, the outline of a bow into a single swan's wing into a clock that had upon it not one mark of *time* – unless a blue cloud passed. But the cloud would pass on, and time was over, meaningless and gone. Only the changes of the moon told time, but this was in circles: bow to wing to orb to wing to bow to wing... And on the changeable shape of the moon might only be played, as on an instrument of great worth, a song to break – and mend – the hearts of any that might hear it.

Oh gods, oh God, oh any that may listen – listen then. That *Then* was Yesterday. When time shifted in a circle and dragons flew and snakes cast off their skins and were maidens and heroes, and stars were born, and love changed but never died, and we were young, and miracles were possible.

Come, walk on the waters of our lives, view these deserts and dead seas, these broken mountains and these far abyssal depths that hold not even a single bone, let alone a tempting devil –

Linardien, Simyo and Ulvad will pitch their high-tech camp beside the edge of a dry ocean, now a psychic tip.
    Simyo will look upward, her dark, sensibly cropped hair, which on the long journey has managed to grow a little, like a naughty child, will stir in a faint breeze that is real, and therefore scentless, textureless and nearly lifeless.
    Simyo will suddenly see a sparkling palace, set some five miles out from shore on what after all appears to be a lake. The palace will have (had) glowing windows, and enormous sails which, when the palace, or the palace's inheritors desire, will move it like a ship.
    But the palace, like dragons and giant doves, sorcerers, antique seas and lakes, will be by this future date, un-existent. It, they, will be gone. They will be gon*ed*.
    Simyo will weep then, without tears. Simyo will be – and is – by then a pragmatist.
    The past will have to die, for the ghost of the past, with all its glory of sorcery and glamour and loveliness, impairs this barren future. How, in whatever Nameless-as-it-will-be name, can anything build up again, form and flower and prosper, unless all such lies as were the Ghost of Yesterday Past are – is – will be – destroyed?
    One must not live on memories.
    One shalt not, *will* not, (though may slightly, somewhat), hold fast to dreams of former times.
    Now the moon will *not* change. Will not even rise.
    Now we will all be *bold* and *face* the *facts*. We will forget and leave the sand in which we buried our heads. (The sweet cool-warm gentle sand, kind as a kiss.) We will be strong and clever,

and have no hearts.

Ulvad will emerge at this point from out of a technologically infallible tent, stoically heated and ultra clean, with carefully chemically sterilised bitter water, and nourishing, un-fattening, tasteless food, and wise sexual aids that elevate the art of making love into a nonsense, and orgasm into a sensible duty. Ulvad will stand there, in the tent's mouth, and politely inquire if Simyo might return with him inside said tent.

There will be no moon like a bow, a lute, a mandolin, a violin, a mirror, a clock, to say No.

Yes, of course, will say the night, empty of reason and of stars.

Or *no, no, no, no, not THIS way* will say the vanished stars, (like diamond jewellery of another jewelled time, before the wonderfully scientific and most excellently tempered future-tomorrow-laws will destroy them, and it all). No, No, No, will say those stars. But Man cannot stand very much Unreality – Man, getting the message wrong, as 'Man' will do. Imagination, says the insanity of misunderstanding, must and will die. We will and must face the future.

God help us all, though God will be dead too.

Tomorrow and tomorrow and tomorrow.

Oh, Yesterday.

"Oh, yes, then," will courteously answer Simyo. And Ulvad will go back into the techno-tent, and Simyo will follow, for a strict half hour of the sexual act. *Act* being the valid word.

And Linardien meanwhile will walk about the hills.

How closed will be the dark, since the dragons and giant birds, the sorcerers and other wonders, and the moon, stars, seas and all heaven-on-earth will have departed.

Linardien will have a secret.

Linardien will look, and look, hoping for some sudden otherness.

Until –

Over a hill, cat-fur dark with pines and eucalyptus, the Phoenix lifted. Burning bright. Up and up the Phoenix flew. Whoever had seen such luminescence would know the Phoenix was *true* fire. But more than fire, the Phoenix rose and had risen and will rise – from ashes.

Linardien wept, but he did not comprehend his tears.

Ulvad and Simyo lay athletically together in the clever tent.

It was their task, these three travellers, to exorcise – *destroy* – by their mere technically and logically tinted (polluted) progress through such lands – all the old dreams, the supernatural alchemic imaginative visions of Yesterday, and the ghosts of Yesterday. Nevertheless, even so, once or twice, now and then, here and there, up and down, in and out...

...they did not.

Seeing the Phoenix, Linardien cried salt tears, which fell like silver drops, which fell, which fall, which shall fall – upward into heaven.

How else, indeed, for fuck's fucking fuck-sake, will we ever get back the God-remembering stars?

Yesternight

A bride, the Day, in golden flower,
Burned through her life until the violet hour,
When, in the funeral dusk, she sank beyond
The shoulder of the world that she had danced upon.

Then rose her ghost, at silent pace,
In shadow-black, yet lit with eerie grace
By tangling spangles and one coldest, pale,
Thin, clouded lamp, that followed her, but seemed to fail.

The bride becomes the died. Dead day,
A phantom only, left to mourn, to stay
Haunting the earth beneath her pallid light:
The ghost of Yesterday is Yesternight.

When comes tomorrow, up will rise
Another golden girl to light the skies,
Till she too dies, and all the world goes dark,
And Day's black widow, Night, weeps out each star.

Publishing History

Ablan
Original to this collection

The Abortionist's Horse – *Dark Terrors 5: The Gollancz Book of Horror*, ed. by Stephen Jones and David Sutton, Gollancz, UK, 2001
The Year's Best Fantasy And Horror: Fourteenth Annual Collection, edited by Ellen Datlow and Terri Windling, USA, 2001.

Blue Vase of Ghosts
Dragonfields: Tales of Fantsy no. 4 magazine, ed. by Charles de Lint and Charles Saunders, Canada, Winter 1983
The Year's Best Fantasy Stories 10, ed. by Arthur W Saha, USA DAW, 1983
Top Fantasy, ed. by Josh Pachter, Dent, UK, 1985
Nightshades: Thirteen Journeys into Shadow, Tanith Lee, Headline, UK, 1993

The Ghost (In Two Letters)
Hauntings, ed. by Ian Whates, Newcon Press, UK, 2012

The Ghost of the Clock
The Dark: New Ghost Stories, ed. by Ellen Datlow, Tor, USA, 2004

The Lady-Of-Shalott House
Realms of Fantasy, Vol 4, no. 1, USA, October 1997
Tempting the Gods: The Selected Stories of Tanith Lee, Volume One, Wildside Press, USA, 2009

The Minstrel's Tale
Invitation to Camelot: An Arthurian Anthology of Short Stories, ed. by Parke Godwin, Ace, USA, 1988

A Night on the Hill
After Hours, Volume 2, No. 3, USA, Summer 1990

Seeing, Believing
Original to this collection

The Sky Won't Listen
Sky Whales and Other Wonders, ed. by Vera Nazarian, Norilana Books, USA, 2009

The Squire's Tale
Sorcerer's Apprentice 7, USA, Summer 1980   *Women as Demons: The Male Perception of Women Through Space and Time*, stories by Tanith Lee, The Women's Press, UK, 1989

Tan
The Immersion Book of SF, ed. by Carmelo Rafala, Immersion Press, UK, 2010

Thuvia Made of Mars
Original to this collection

The Winter Ghosts
Weird Tales – No. 303 (Vol 53, No. 2, Winter 1991/92 (USA)
100 Fiendish Little Frightmares, ed. by Stefan Dziemianowicz, Robert Weinberg & Martin H Greenberg, Barnes and Noble, USA, 1997

Yesterday
Original to this collection

Yesternight
Original to this collection

About the Author

Tanith Lee was born in North London (UK) in 1947. Because her parents were professional dancers (ballroom, Latin American) and had to live where the work was, she attended a number of truly terrible schools, and didn't learn to read – she is also dyslectic – until almost age 8. And then only because her father taught her. This opened the world of books to Lee, and by 9 she was writing. After much better education at a grammar school, Lee went on to work in a library. This was followed by various other jobs – shop assistant, waitress, clerk – plus a year at art college when she was 25-26. In 1974 this mosaic ended when DAW Books of America, under the leadership of Donald A Wollheim, bought and published Lee's *The Birthgrave*, and thereafter 26 of her novels and collections.

Since then Lee has written around 95 books, and over 300 short stories. 4 of her radio plays have been broadcast by the BBC; she also wrote 2 episodes (*Sarcophagus* and *Sand*) for the TV series *Blake's 7*. Some of her stories regularly get read on Radio 4 Extra.

Lee writes in many styles in and across many genres, including Horror, SF and Fantasy, Historical, Detective, Contemporary-Psychological, Children and Young Adult. Her preoccupation, though, is always people.

In 1992 she married the writer-artist-photographer John Kaiine, her companion since 1987. They live on the Sussex Weald, near the sea, in a house full of books and plants, with two black and white overlords called cats.

NewCon Press
http://newconpress.co.uk/

The very best in fantasy, science fiction, and horror

Colder Greyer Stones by Tanith Lee

Released to commemorate the author being honoured with a Lifetime Achievement Award at the 2013 World Fantasy Convention, this stunning collection of stories provides further evidence of why Tanith Lee is held in such high regard by fans and contemporaries alike. The book features twelve wonderful, rich-textured tales including the brand new novelette "The Frost Watcher" and five stories previously available only in the (sold out) signed limited edition "Cold Grey Stones".

Paperback: ISBN 978-1-907069-60-4   £9.99

The Moon King by Neil Williamson

"Beautifully written and thoughtful… one of the best debuts of this or any other year." – *Jeff Vandermeer*

"The Moon King is literary fantasy at its best." – *The Guardian*

Life under the moon has always been predictable: day follows night, wax phases to wane and, after the despair of every Darkday, a person's mood soars to euphoria at Full. So it has been for the five hundred years since Glassholm was founded, but now all that has changed. Amidst rumours of unsettling dreams and strange whispering children, society is disintegrating into unrest and violence. Three people find themselves at the eye of the storm: a former policeman investigating a series of macabre murders, an artist embroiled in the intrigues of revolution, and a renegade engineer tasked with fixing the ancient machine at the city's heart…

Paperback: ISBN 978-1-907069-62-8   £12.99

Other Immanion Press Titles by Tanith Lee
The Colouring Book Series

Greyglass 9781907737046 £10.99
The house... always growing, adding to itself, blooming, decaying, becoming reborn... But Susan doesn't live in the house of Catherine, her grandmother. When Catherine dies, no one mourns. The house is always changing. As if at last it must achieve some irresistible transformation. Frankly, there is something *uncanny* about the house. Isn't there.

To Indigo 9781907737213 £11.99
Don't talk to strangers. Don't even look at them. Novelist Roy Phipps leads an uneventful existence in the house inherited from his parents. His only aberration is the story he's been secretively writing for years of the mad poet Vilmos, a study of murder, angst and alchemic magic. Then one evening Roy meets Vilmos, face to face. As shadows close in on him, Roy understands he's now fighting for his own sanity. And probably his life.

L'Amber 9781907737251 £11.99
Jay has very little. Jilaine Best has everything. But even Jilane's perfect life is flawed, longing for the baby she's unable to conceive. She's willing to let another woman give birth for her. And so Jay confesses she is already pregnant with an unwanted child. Lies are so easy to tell, if you've had enough practice. Harder to change into truth. Spin your web. Watch it tangle. Now see what you've caught.

Killing Violets 9781907737367 £10.99
1934... Starving to death somewhere in Europe, Anna meets Raoul, who takes her to England and the dubious mansion of his arrogant and unsavoury relatives, the Basultes. Anna is a survivor. Both the aristocratic malignities, and the Hogarthian orgies of the servants, can be accommodated, if they must. Anna has a past as savage and explicit as anything seen in the Basulte house.

Ivoria 9781907737404 £11.99
Nick Lewis certainly has no liking for his TV historian brother, Laurence. Aside from anything else Nick blames him for the death of their mother, the beautiful actress Claudia Martin. And so, is it possible the off-handedly childish trick played by Nick on Laurence really does cast some kind of curse? This is probably *not* a supernatural story. It might be less unsettling if it was.

Cruel Pink 9781907737497 £11.99
Emenie, a serial killer, lives alone. She can read omens and knows exactly her legitimate prey. Rod has a dreary life, working at an unrewarding job with something uneasy hanging over him. Is it the wardrobe? Klova is young, beautiful, living on benign handouts, in a Science Fantasy existence of sprints and liquid-silver...Until she meets the challenging Coal. Here, at the outskirts of this City they all call London, what the Hell is going on?

Turquoiselle 9781907737596 £11.99
Not much is what it seems. The job can be dull, but quite demanding. The work is lucrative, however. He can easily afford the costly wants of Donna, his partner. It's just that suddenly things are running less smoothly. This stuff with Donna... Various unusual tensions at work... the bizarre and threatening business over Silvia... In the end, maybe all you can rely on is yourself.

www.ingramcontent.com/pod-product-compliance
Ingram Content Group UK Ltd.
Pitfield, Milton Keynes, MK11 3LW, UK
UKHW041303180426
11947UKWH00009B/651